End Call

"Nancy, I'm—" *Bloop!*

George's voice was unclear behind the blooping noise. I screamed into the phone, not caring who heard me now; just hoping George would. *"George! There are invoices for lab equipment! I think we're in a research facility! George!"*

"I hear you, Nancy. We're com—" *Bloop!*

"Aaauuugh!" I screamed as a hand suddenly reached out from behind me, grabbed the phone out of my hand, and pressed the End button. Trembling violently I turned around. Anna faced me, her skin pale, her hair wild around her face. She was fully conscious.

"What have you *done*?" she demanded.

D0736172

NANCY DREW

Available from Aladdin Paperbacks

CAROLYN KEENE

NANCY DREW

GIRL DETECTIVE

THE PERFECT ESCAPE #32

**Book Three in the
Perfect Mystery Trilogy**

This book is a work of fiction. Any references to historical events, real people, or real locales are used fictitiously. Other names, characters, places, and incidents are the product of the author's imagination, and any resemblance to actual events or locales or persons, living or dead, is entirely coincidental.

❧ALADDIN PAPERBACKS
An imprint of Simon & Schuster Children's Publishing Division
1230 Avenue of the Americas, New York, NY 10020
Copyright © 2008 by Simon & Schuster, Inc.
All rights reserved, including the right of
reproduction in whole or in part in any form.
NANCY DREW, NANCY DREW: GIRL DETECTIVE, ALADDIN PAPER-
BACKS, and related logo are registered trademarks of Simon & Schuster, Inc.
Manufactured in the United States of America
First Aladdin Paperbacks edition October 2008
10 9 8 7 6 5 4 3 2 1
Library of Congress Control Number 2008920581
ISBN-13: 978-1-4169-5531-3
ISBN-10: 1-4169-5531-3

Contents

DEAD BATTERY

Beep. Beep. Beep. Beep. Beep.

I awoke in darkness. Gulping in a breath of air, I tried not to panic. Where *was* I? Why was I lying on the floor in a strange, dark room? I tried to pull my hands in front of me— Why were my *hands tied?* My pulse raced as adrenalin shot through my system, and I struggled to sit up. Then it all came back to me.

The pageant.

Pretty Face cosmetics.

Kyle McMahon and Adam Bedrossian.

Weeks before, I had entered a regional beauty pageant to investigate a case I was working. To my shock, I had won the pageant—but not before figuring out that the sponsor, Pretty Face cosmetics, had something to hide. A few days ago, Bess, George and I had flown to New York City for the national pageant. While there, I had met a local Pretty Face employee, Anna Chavez—a scientist. It was Anna who led me to find out Pretty Face was marketing a product that contained an untested substance that might lead to paralysis.

Before Anna and I had time to talk about anything, she had mysteriously gone missing. When I went looking for Anna at Pretty Face's headquarters, I had walked into a trap. It was obviously because I knew too much, and Kyle McMahon and Adam Bedrossian, a Pretty Face bigwig and head of security, respectively, wanted to keep me quiet.

They had taken Anna, and then me, captive and loaded us into a helicopter. That was the last thing I remembered: rising up over the gorgeous skyline of Manhattan, wondering what on Earth these two men were going to do with us. They must have used something to knock us out—chloroform, maybe?—so we wouldn't see where we were headed.

And now here I was.

"Hello?" I called, and my voice came out husky

from disuse. No one answered. There wasn't even a sound. Except . . .

Beep. Beep. Beep. Beep. Beep.

Suddenly I realized . . . that quiet, electronic beeping. It had been going on for a while now, and was probably what woke me up in the first place. But where was it coming from?

Was Anna here with me? Or had Kyle and Adam separated us?

She hadn't answered when I called out, but maybe she was still unconscious.

Either way I wasn't going to be able to find her by lying on the floor. I sat up, struggling with my bonds. My hands and feet were both bound with what felt like duct tape. I wiggled and squirmed and finally managed to loosen the tape around my ankles, but it wasn't coming off completely. I needed something sharp to snag it on. I very carefully got my balance and pulled myself to my feet. I hopped around clumsily, making my way forward. Eventually I hit something that felt like a wall.

Now that my eyes had adjusted to the darkness, I could see that a tiny shaft of light was coming in through a corner of a blacked-out window. If I really concentrated, I could make out the vague shapes of furniture. There was a wire storage shelf along the wall, like something you'd find in someone's garage, just a few feet away from me. The ends of the wires were sharp-looking. I hopped over, then pressed the bond on my wrists against the exposed edges, over and over again.

First I poked a small hole in the tape, and finally, with a lot of effort, cut through the tape completely. With a sigh of relief, I pulled my hand loose—away from the sticky duct tape. With a painful rip, I yanked my hand completely free of the tape. Then I carefully bent down, found the end of the tape around my feet, and ripped off those bonds as well.

Beep. Beep. Beep. Beep. Beep.

It was too quiet to be an alarm. But what could it be? What kind of electronic device might have been left in this room?

"Anna?" I called, but there was still no reply. And even with the tiny shaft of light from the window, it was still too dark to make out anything except the one wall of the mystery prison. I moved toward the beep slowly, quietly as I could, feeling my way along the wall. It was cold and rough, possibly a concrete block, like a school building or a basement. I walked a few feet and, as I moved forward, the beeping got louder. . . .

"Oof!" Just as I felt I was getting close, my foot hit something soft and warm. It startled me so much, I jumped about a foot in the air and almost went flying over it. My recent pageant win notwithstanding, nobody would ever accuse me of being graceful. I knelt down and felt around for whatever I'd hit.

It moved immediately beneath my fingertips. It was a knee! I squinted hard at the shape and relief washed over me at the sight.

"Anna!" I cried. "Anna, are you all right? Wake up!"

I took Anna by the shoulders and shook her, but she didn't respond. Bending close to her mouth, I could feel and hear that she was breathing at a normal pace. She still seemed to be unconscious, though. Moving her knee must have been an unconscious reflex.

Beep. Beep. Beep.

The noise was louder still, as though it were coming from Anna herself. Could Anna have smuggled something in? Something electronic that might help us make contact with the outside world? Listening carefully, I tried to follow the sound. It was coming from her pants pocket . . . No . . . Her knee? . . . No . . . I leaned down farther.

It was coming from her *foot*.

"What is going *on*?" I muttered, gamely leaning over and pulling off Anna's left sneaker. I shook the shoe: nothing. The beep was definitely coming from her foot. *Am I dealing with the bionic woman here?* I reached over, felt that Anna was still wearing a sock, and pulled that off. Just then, something square-shape and shiny dropped to the floor.

Beep. Beep. Beep. Beep. Beep.

I picked up the source of the beeping, brushing one of its tiny buttons by accident.

A large, square screen illuminated.

HI ANNA! SATURDAY, 2:37P.M. EST. YOU HAVE 2 MISSED CALLS. DETECTING WI-FI CONNECTION. MORE INFO?

It was a phone!

Actually, it was more than a phone. It was a full-service PDA—Internet access and all. I wasn't too familiar with the newfangled things, but my friend George had gotten one recently and given Bess and I a lecture on how powerful it was and how it meant she could "connect to anyone, anything, any Web site, any source of information at any time!"

I felt my heart quicken. The Internet, plus a phone! We were saved! Thank goodness for

Anna's quick thinking—and her thick, baggy socks!

I pressed the button that promised more info. A window popped up:

NONE OF YOUR TRUSTED WI-FI NETWORKS ARE AVAILABLE. WOULD YOU LIKE TO CONNECT TO THE OPEN NETWORK HYUNGKOO43?

Hyungkoo43. *Save me, Hyungkoo43, you're my only hope!* "Yes, yes, *yes!*" I whispered, pressing the button for OK. Immediately an Internet window popped up, leading me to a popular search engine. I was connected! And I had a *phone!*

I started dialing George's number before the search engine page was fully loaded. As her phone rang, I looked around and peered at what I could see of the room, realizing that I had one problem.

Sure, I had access to any friend whose phone number I had memorized and any piece of information that was available on the Web. What I *didn't* have was any idea as to my whereabouts. I could beg George to come save us, but I couldn't give her the faintest clue as to where to find us.

I took a quick look around the room, or, at least, what I could see of it. It looked like some kind of storage room. There were a few utility shelves, like the one I'd cut the tape on, but there wasn't much furniture; just some boxes and random office equipment. Based on the position of the blacked-out window—it was way at the top of the wall—I guessed we were probably in a basement somewhere.

Ring. Ring. Ring. My heart quickened. *Come on, George,* I thought. *Pick up!* Anna's number wouldn't be programmed into George's phone, so she'd think a total stranger was calling her, possibly a wrong number. Would she let the phone go to voice mail? Did she even know I was missing yet? I had no idea how long I'd been out for.

"Hello?"

A rush of relief flooded through me at the sound of George's familiar but slightly hesitant voice.

"George!" I cried. "It's me!"

"Nancy?" George sounded confused. "Where *are* you? And whose phone are you calling from?"

"Anna's," I said quickly. "Listen, George, you have to help me. Where are you?"

"Bess and I are back at the hotel," George said, panic evident in her voice. "Nancy, you're scaring me—Tell me where you are!"

"It's all gone wrong," I admitted. "I found

Anna, she was being held by Kyle and Adam at the Pretty Face offices downtown. But the two of them were there too. It was a setup!"

"Oh my god," George said breathlessly. "Are they there now? Nancy, are you safe?"

"No, I don't see them. I don't know if I'm safe, maybe—" I was about to continue, but the phone let out an ear-curdling *bloop*.

"What's that?" I asked, sure that George would speak the language of any electronic device.

"Nancy? Are you there?"

I started to panic. "George?!" Was I losing her?

"Nancy, your phone is beeping. It sounds like Anna's phone is dying. Just quickly tell me: Where are you?"

I felt my heart sink. "I don't know," I replied, trying to stay calm. "They gave us something to knock us out and took us in a helicopter. We're in a basement storage room of some kind."

Bloop. Anna's phone let out another depressing sound.

George was quiet for a minute. I could tell she was beginning to feel as afraid for me as I felt for myself. "Nancy," she replied. "Think. Do you remember anything about where you were headed in the helicopter?"

My heart was pounding. I tried to take a deep

breath to slow it. "I don't know New York City very well," I replied, "but I think we were heading north—up the East River."

George was silent. That only left the entire state of New York, plus Connecticut. I could tell she was despairing of ever finding us. And honestly, so was I.

Bloop.

"Listen carefully," George said. "Do you hear anything from outside? City noises? Animals? Anything?"

I fell silent. For a second I couldn't hear anything but my own pounding heart. But then I could hear cars passing, the slamming of a car door. A siren, somewhere far in the distance. It was the sound of the city. . . . Something I had almost grown immune to in the short time I'd been in New York.

"I hear city noise," I replied. "I think we're right on the street. And . . ." I paused. I heard something else, but I couldn't believe it. It made no sense with the cars passing and the noise of traffic . . .

"What is it?" George asked. "Hurry, Nance, if your phone's dying, we don't have much time."

Bawk. Bawk, bawk, bawk. "Chickens," I said, disbelief still lingering in my voice. "I know it's crazy, George, but I hear them clear as day. Live chickens."

Bloop.

Silence for a moment. I could tell George was as thrown for a loop as I was. "Is there anything else?"

Suddenly I remembered. "One thing. Hold on." I held the phone away from my ear to double-check the screen. "Okay," I said, putting the phone back into position. "I'm picking up a Wi-Fi signal on Anna's PDA. The name of the network is Hyungkoo43." I spelled it.

"Hyungkoo43," George repeated, and I could hear her writing it down. "Anything else? Any papers in the room, identifying objects?"

Papers. I hastily got to my feet and felt my way back to the wire shelving. There was a box of files there. I quickly opened the top and grabbed as many folders as I could. Throwing them down on the floor, I pawed through the pages, but it was too dark to read what they said. Quickly, I pulled the phone away from my ear and shone the light from the screen onto the papers.

Bloop.

"Nancy! *Nancy!*" I could hear George yelling even with the phone down by my knees. I brought it back against my ear.

"Yes?"

"Nancy, I'm—" *Bloop.*

George's voice was unclear behind the blooping noise. I screamed into the phone, not caring who heard me now; just hoping George would. *"George! There are invoices for lab equipment! I think we're in a research facility! George!"*

"I hear you, Nancy. We're com—" *Bloop!*

"Aaauuugh!" I screamed as a hand suddenly reached out from behind me, grabbed the phone out of my hand, and pressed the End button. Trembling violently I turned around. Anna faced me, her skin pale, her hair wild around her face. She was fully conscious.

"What have you *done?*" she demanded.

ALARMED

Anna stared at the phone in her hand, pressing buttons and frowning deeply. "What did you do, Nancy? Who did you call?"

"Anna?" I reached out to touch my new friend's shoulder, trying to speak in soothing tones. "Are you okay? Do you remember what happened?"

Anna shifted and pushed my hand away. Her expression was dead serious, her eyes wide. "Nancy. Listen to me. Who. Did. You. Call."

I didn't understand. Calling George had been our only hope. Why did Anna seem so angry? "I called my friend George. I hoped maybe she could help find us. She's a whiz with computers, and—"

But Anna was already moaning. "Oh no." She shook her head and closed her eyes, turning the phone off. "No, no, no . . ."

"What is it?" I asked. What on Earth could be wrong? I thought maybe Anna was wary of strangers, or maybe she thought George would tell the wrong person what had happened. But of course I knew George would be careful and could be trusted with anything. Maybe once I convinced Anna of that, she would calm down.

Anna shook her head one last time and opened her eyes. She looked at me with a frank, unapologetic expression. "That phone was given to me by Pretty Face cosmetics," she said flatly. "They can track all of my calls, all of my activity. Now that you've made a phone call, they'll know that we're awake, that we have a phone, and that we've called someone for help."

My face paled. "That means . . . someone is probably on their way to us right now."

Anna nodded. "And not just us. Whoever you called, Nancy, could be in grave danger."

I felt my heart stop for a few seconds. *George and Bess.* Was it possible that by calling on them for help, I'd put a very dangerous person on their trail? They were at the hotel where all the pageant participants were staying, surrounded by contestants and Pretty Face bigwigs. It would be so easy for Pretty Face to send someone up to their room . . .

I grabbed the phone back. "I have to call George," I said, hitting Redial before Anna could stop me. The time on the phone now read 2:50 p.m.—five hours until the pageant started. "I have to warn her. . . ."

But the phone just gave one dispiriting *bloop* before going dark altogether.

Adrenaline surged through my veins. I shook the phone, then rammed it hard against the floor. "Come on!" I cried. "Just one more minute of juice . . . Just thirty seconds . . . I have to warn George!"

After a few seconds of banging the phone against the ground, Anna reached out and put her hand on my arm. "Nancy," she said. "It's too late. The battery is dead."

I looked at her, not wanting to believe it. Knowing I was trapped in some basement while my best friends in the world might be in danger was too much for me. I looked around the room again, searching for an exit, any exit.

"The window!"

I stood up, pointing to the blacked-out rectangle on the side of the room. "If we could break it with something heavy . . ."

Anna looked doubtful. "Nancy, we have to be careful. If we break the window, who knows what might happen? We could trigger an alarm. . . ."

I whirled around. "Who *cares*?" I asked. "By the time they got here, we'd be long gone. And you just said they're probably on their way anyway."

Anna frowned. And I could identify another emotion playing on her face: fear. "They're already angry," she murmured nervously. "Anything else we do . . ."

"Exactly," I said, fumbling over to the wire shelves and lifting the first solid, heavy object I found. It felt like a printer or a fax machine. "They're *already* angry. So we can't make it any worse. And, best-case scenario, we get out of here."

Anna still looked doubtful.

"We have to at least try," I pleaded.

Anna frowned. But she stood up, wordlessly coming to my side and walking with me to the window. She grabbed one side of the printer/fax.

"Should we just throw it up there?" she asked, looking warily at the window.

I lifted my side of the machine up a couple of

inches, trying to get a good grip on it. "We've got to kind of bash it into the window," I replied. "But we have to do it *hard*. Ready?"

Anna still looked nervous, but she nodded. "Ready."

"One . . . two . . . three!"

The crash shattered the silence: splintering glass, metal on metal, and then the dejected crash of the printer falling to the ground. And finally the *whoo, whoo, whoo* of an alarm system. Anna had been right; we'd triggered something.

"It worked!" I cried as soon as I spotted sunlight. "We're fr—"

But we weren't. The glass was shattered and sunlight poured into the room, but it also illuminated another security feature: bars. Bars covered the outside of the window, making it impossible for anyone to break in—or out.

"Oh *no*," Anna moaned, shaking her head. "Oh, I don't know how I could have been so stupid. Most city buildings wouldn't leave a ground-floor window unprotected."

I blinked, trying desperately to look on the bright side. "Maybe that means we're still in New York?"

Anna just kept shaking her head. I sighed, looking out the window. We didn't seem to be on a busy street, as I'd hoped. It looked as though we were facing some sort of driveway, close enough to hear the street, but not to see it.

Whoo, whoo, whoo, whoo. The alarm was maddening. I closed my eyes and put my fingers to my temples, trying to calm myself. It was all I could do not to picture some scary guy grabbing Bess and George off the street, or Adam Bedrossian gunning through midday traffic to get to us and punish us for what we'd done.

"Anna," I said, "please, before they come, tell me what happened at Pretty Face."

Anna looked back at me like I was crazy. "Now?" she asked.

"We don't have many options," I said, gesturing around the newly illuminated but still securely locked room. "And I could use a distraction right now, to keep from thinking about my friends' safety. Okay?"

Anna still looked skeptical, but she seemed to understand what I was saying. "Okay." We looked around and eventually settled down on the floor away from the broken window glass.

"Start at the beginning, and tell me your side of the story," I said.

Anna looked thoughtful through the obvious apprehension. "I started working at Pretty Face three years ago," she began. "I was a big fan of their products, and I was happy to land the job. For the first couple years, everything was lovely. But about six months into my first year, I heard that they were experimenting with a toxin from the *unibro* frog."

I nodded. "And you'd heard of this frog?"

Anna nodded. "It hails from my country, Venezuela. And I knew that the indigenous people in my country used ingredients from the frog in different folk remedies."

"Folk remedies for what?" I asked.

Anna shrugged. "Sore muscles, arthritis, those sorts of things," she replied. "Simple pain. The frog excretes a neurotoxin from its skin that causes paralysis to those who try to eat it. The neurotoxin can make minor pain more bearable."

I nodded. "But you said earlier that you were concerned about Pretty Face using the toxin. Why?"

Anna frowned. "In my country, people are very careful not to use the toxin too often. And they never apply it to the face."

"Why?" I asked.

Anna shook her head. "I've heard stories that it can be deadly if you use it too often and over a long period of time. That's why people in my country use it sparingly, carefully."

I nodded slowly. Pretty Face was using the toxin in their new facial moisturizer and revitalizer, Perfect Face, something that girls and women would apply daily. I had actually worn it for the local pageant I'd won. It caused a strange tingly sensation that I didn't like. In fact, I was first alerted to the fact that Pretty Face was up to something shady when I realized that my new friend Kelly, Kyle McMahon's daughter, had been given an older formula of Perfect Face, one that didn't tingle. I now realized that Kyle had been protecting his daughter from the toxin he knew might be dangerous.

"Did you tell the people at Pretty Face that you were concerned?" I asked.

Whoo, whoo.

The alarm continued to clang in the background. Its shrill shriek never sounded any less annoying or terrifying, no matter how long it went on for.

Anna nodded. "Of course I did. I'm a researcher, Nancy. I didn't tell them they should flat-out stop using the toxin. I told them I wanted to do a study—a scientific study to make sure that the toxin had no harmful long-term effects. But such a study would take many years to do correctly—

ten, at least. Nobody at Pretty Face wanted to wait that long to get Perfect Face on the market. See, other cosmetics companies were also looking at the toxin, and Pretty Face wanted to be the first to sell products containing it. They'd invested lots of money into developing Perfect Face, and they didn't want to let their big payoff go to another company."

I nodded. "And when they told you that, you still didn't feel comfortable keeping quiet about the toxin."

Anna shrugged. "No. I asked them to, at the very least, let me go to Venezuela and interview the indigenous people. If I couldn't do a scientific study, I could get some firsthand accounts of what the toxin does. But they didn't even let me do that. I think they were afraid of getting unfavorable accounts, Nancy. If they heard even one negative story about the frog toxin, then they couldn't play dumb anymore. Without a study or the interviews, Pretty Face can claim they weren't warned, they had no idea the toxin might be harmful."

"But you did warn them," I pointed out.

Anna nodded, holding her temples with her fingertips as though they would shield her from the continuous screeching of the alarm. "I found an article from a South American scientific journal. It said that the toxin was likely to have harmful long-term affects, but further study was needed."

I nodded vigorously. "I found that article in your desk when I was looking for clues about your disappearance!"

Anna smiled ruefully. "I showed it to my boss, but he didn't take it seriously. He said the journal I'd gotten the article from wasn't well-respected. He took it from me—right out of my hands—and we never discussed it again. I had another copy, but he didn't know that. And it didn't matter. I was so happy to have a good job, I backed down. For a year or so, I was quiet about the toxin. But then I came to the pageant, and I saw all these young girls using Pretty Face. It stirred my conscience. After the protesters disrupted the rehearsal the other night—"

"You brought up the subject with your boss again?" I supplied.

Anna nodded. "I told Kyle McMahon that it was time to come clean. I told him that people would be paying attention now, and if Pretty Face confessed before anyone pointed any fingers at them, it would make the company look like they were at least taking responsiblity. But he told me it wasn't possible. Not only would they do no further research into the toxin, they were actually using the pageant to kick off a multimillion-dollar marketing campaign—to teenagers."

"I can't believe that," I murmured. I knew something shady was going on at Pretty Face, but marketing a product that might cause paralysis to *teenagers* was even lower than I'd thought the company was capable of doing.

I was suddenly aware of the fact that the alarm had stopped. Anna and I looked at each other for a moment, both of us probably realizing at the same moment that this could either help us or be a very bad omen that the bad guys were on their way or—worse—already here. I decided I couldn't focus on that right now—neither of us could. "Go on," I urged Anna.

"I was furious, Nancy," Anna went on, her eyes sweeping the dark corners of the room before settling back on me. "How could I work for a company that has so little concern for its customers? Was a steady paycheck worth not being able to sleep at night? I thought long and hard on it, and I decided that I had to do something. I had to tell the world what Pretty Face was up to. But I needed help."

I frowned. *Help?* This was new. I knew Anna had gotten into trouble for telling Pretty Face her concerns about the frog toxin, but I didn't know she'd had help.

Anna looked at me carefully. "You were a contestant in the pageant. You must know Piper Depken."

My eyes widened. "*Piper?!*" I cried. I knew Piper all right—I'd even come close to considering her a friend until she got too close to the crown and turned into a vindictive, paranoid, ultracompetitive nut. What on Earth was *she* doing helping Anna? Granted, she hated Pretty Face cosmetics, but only because they'd given me the regional crown and not her. I couldn't imagine that she'd ruin her chances of taking my place as runner-up by hurting Pretty Face's image in any way.

But Anna was already shaking her head. "No, no. Not Piper. Piper's sister. Robin Depken."

Robin. Of course. I knew Robin too. In the process of investigating the case that led me to all this—the dethroning of the last reigning Miss Pretty Face—I'd come across Robin, the bitter first runner-up in last year's competition who'd been stripped of her position after a judge admitted to fixing her scores. Robin hated Pretty Face more than anyone, and had even told me at one point that she wouldn't let their products touch her face. She only let Piper compete in this year's pageant because she knew Piper could use the scholarship prize.

"Yes, I've met Robin," I said simply. "But how did you meet her?"

Anna looked uncomfortable. "I got to know her at last year's national pageant," she admitted. "She is majoring in biochemistry like I did. She seemed very down-to-earth compared to the other girls. We struck up a friendship. I took her to my favorite boutiques around the city, and after the pageant, we stayed in touch by e-mail."

I nodded. "You told her about the frog toxin?"

Anna sighed. "Maybe I shouldn't have. But I was worried, Nancy. I was frustrated that my boss wouldn't listen to me, and more than anything I needed to have someone tell me I wasn't crazy. Especially someone who knew the science of what might happen as a result of the toxin."

"So you told Robin," I said.

"I did. At first I was vague. I told her that I was having trouble at work, that my boss wouldn't listen to me about an issue I felt was very important. Then, finally, I forwarded her an e-mail I'd gotten from my boss, telling me to forget the frog-toxin issue, that Pretty Face was choosing not to follow up on it."

My mouth dropped open. "And?"

Anna looked sheepish. "And I didn't hear from her again," she admitted. "When I saw her again at this year's pageant—escorting her sister—I invited her to lunch. She confessed to me then that she had used my e-mail to try to blackmail Pretty Face into dethroning the reigning Miss Pretty Face and giving her the crown."

I gasped. "What!" I cried. "*She* dethroned Portia? What on Earth—?" When I'd worked on Portia Leoni's case, I had eventually learned that Portia blackmailed one of her competitors into dropping out of the pageant, and I'd concluded that the competitor had used her influence to frame Portia for shoplifting—and get her dethroned. Had I been wrong?

Anna shook her head. "She underestimated Pretty Face if she thought they would give up so easily," she replied. "Pretty Face would not be blackmailed. Instead of installing Robin as the new Miss Pretty Face, they did dethrone Portia—but more because she was a nuisance than anything else—and then they stripped Robin of her position, too, just to show her that they wouldn't be bullied by her threats. The e-mail I'd forwarded looked shady, but it didn't contain enough information for her to interest the press or anyone else. Her plan backfired."

I shook my head, trying to absorb all of this new information. "Okay. So *Robin* was responsible for getting Portia dethroned—and for getting herself kicked out, as well." I paused, suddenly flashing back on the moment I'd accused Portia's other competitor—Fallon—of getting Portia dethroned. Fallon had cried and cried, insisting that she was innocent, but I had proof—or so I thought. It looked like I'd been wrong all this time. Fallon had been a bit of a prickly personality herself, but I still felt terrible.

"Robin was embarrassed," Anna went on. "After she tried to blackmail Pretty Face with my e-mail, she was too ashamed to contact me again. But during our lunch, we renewed our friendship. She seemed to take an honest interest in my struggles with the frog toxin. She seemed so sincere, I flat-out asked her: If I had evidence to show the world that Pretty Face was endangering their customers, would she help me? And she said yes."

"Robin agreed to help you," I said, still not quite believing it. "So what happened?"

"I went straight from our lunch to my office,"

Anna replied. "I immediately uploaded every e-mail or memo that I had written on the subject onto two flash drives: one for Robin and one for myself. Not just my own writings, but the responses I'd gotten from the higher-ups. Together, the correspondence painted a pretty dire picture for Pretty Face cosmetics. They proved that Pretty Face had been made aware of the potential dangers of using the frog toxin and that they had chosen not to do anything."

I nodded. "And?" I prodded.

"The next morning, I met Robin for breakfast and gave her a flash drive. I planned to alert the press that day, and Robin's files would be my backup, in case anything happened to my drive or to my work computer."

"Okay," I said slowly, still trying to understand what had happened. "So then you went to the press . . . ?"

"No." Anna shook her head vigorously. "Nancy, I never got that far. Within half an hour of giving Robin her flash drive, I was attacked. I was walking from the subway station to my office when a man jumped out of a town car, grabbed me, and pulled me inside. He pushed a rag over my mouth, and the next thing I remember is waking up in the Pretty Face corporate office. Tied up and groggy. And then you found me there."

I shook my head, stunned, trying to make sense of it all. "Wait a minute," I said. "You gave the flash drive to Robin—and within half an hour you were kidnapped? What reason would Robin have to betray you?"

Anna shrugged. "I'm not even sure she did, Nancy. I wasn't careful enough about hiding my actions or my feelings about the toxin. It's possible that Pretty Face was following me, and decided to stop me themselves."

"Did you tell anyone else that you were going to the press?" I asked. "Anyone other than Robin?"

Anna shook her head. "I trusted Robin," she replied. "But perhaps it was a mistake."

I was quiet. Robin was bitter about the pageant when I spoke to her back in River Heights, but I couldn't imagine why she would agree to help Anna, and then betray her. Unless it had to do with money. . . . Robin and Piper's family struggled with money, and Robin had been very honest with me about her need for the prize money that came with the Miss Pretty Face crown. Could Robin have betrayed Anna in the hopes of selling her secrets back to Pretty Face?

Suddenly the sound of a car's rumbling engine approached from around the side of the building and the vehicle parking in what I assumed was the rear, where the broken window faced. My heart thumped in my chest as Anna faced me with a wide-eyed look.

We had company.

But who would it be? I knew I'd given George a bizarre assortment of puzzle pieces to put together—basement, chickens, Hyungkoo43, city. I knew, deep down, that it would be nearly impossible for her to figure out where were and get to us in the tiny amount of time that had elapsed. I also knew that because I had called her on Anna's phone, she might be facing some Pretty Face goons of her own. Still, I couldn't help but hope against hope to hear George's voice on the other side of the door. Either George had found us just in time . . . or this adventure was about to take a very dangerous turn.

The car door slammed. Anna and I looked at each other. We could have easily gotten up and moved to look out the broken window, but I think we were both too terrified to move. Anna bit her lip. I reached over and took her hand. The sound of footsteps walked across a paved surface and then disappeared. A few seconds later we heard them approaching the heavy, locked door near the wire shelves.

Keys. The jingle of someone picking the right one, placing it into the lock. The lock mechanism shifted, metal against metal, something that would normally barely register but that sounded deafening in the silence.

The heavy door swung open.

"Well, well, well." Adam Bedrossian stood in the doorway, framed by fluorescent lights in the hallway behind him. He smiled an evil smile. "Managed to sneak your PDA in here, eh, Anna? How very *Veronica Mars* of you."

I turned to Anna and gulped.

What was Adam about to do to us?

What had become of Bess and George?

And . . . who was Veronica Mars?

CAUGHT ON CAMERA

Adam moved into the storage room, still with the same cold smile on his face. "Did you really think you could get away from us?" he asked, looking from Anna to me. "Get your friends here and, what, break out of the basement? Run to the cops, have us arrested, happily ever after?"

I looked at Anna and swallowed. Adam's eyes looked as hard and black as coal.

"Pretty Face cosmetics has many allies in the NYPD," he went on coolly. "One phone call, and I could be there to pick you girls up. Until this pageant is over and the new Perfect Face campaign is kicked off, you girls had better get used to my company."

"What happened to Bess and George?" I demanded. I felt so frozen, it surprised me to hear my own voice. But I had to know.

"Bess and George," Adam responded, lingering over my friends' names. "Bess and George. Ah yes. I think it's better that you don't know."

A sharp blade of fear pierced my stomach. "What did you do to them?" I demanded, my voice rising in pitch. "Where are they?"

But Adam just waved his hand as though he wouldn't entertain my questions any longer. "You and your friends are very lucky that Kyle McMahon is in charge," he said simply.

"Why?" asked Anna.

"Because Kyle has a daughter your age," Adam replied as though it were obvious. "He has some sympathy for you. If it were up to me . . ."

He didn't finish the sentence. He didn't have to. My insides already felt like ice.

Adam stepped forward and held out his hand. "The phone, please."

Anna glanced at me and then pulled it out of her pocket, where she'd stashed it. "The battery is dead," she explained in a pleading voice.

"Look, we pose no danger to you. We can't contact anyone. If you leave us here, we promise to behave—"

"QUIET!" Adam bellowed, taking the phone and, in one quick motion, dropping it to the cement floor and crushing it under his foot. Even though the battery was dead, I cringed to see the phone destroyed—our last, and only, connection to the outside world was gone.

Adam went on in a low voice. "You didn't only make the phone call. You also broke a window and activated an alarm. Don't try to paint yourselves as a pair of harmless kittens. You are both instigators; troublemakers. If you were capable of behaving, you wouldn't be here in the first place!" He glared at Anna. "*You* don't know when to let something go. Pretty Face hasn't done anything wrong. We have no evidence that the ingredients in Perfect Face have ever done any harm to anyone. So you need to just let it go!"

Then he turned to me. "And you. You're relentless, an instigator of the worst kind. You never know when to leave well enough alone. First, poking around into Portia Leoni's dethroning. You practically uprooted our whole pageant! And then you had to go poking around the Pretty Face offices in New York! Kyle was right to choose you to win the regional pageant, so that we could bring you to New York and keep an eye on you. I only wish we had done something sooner about your snooping!"

I gulped. So *that* was why I'd won the regional pageant. Oh well. I'd had a feeling it wasn't because of my sparkling rendition of "On My Own" from *Les Misérables* or my knack for grace and etiquette.

"What will happen to us now?" Anna asked, and I felt a wave of regret. If only I hadn't snooped around and found Anna's PDA! If I hadn't called George, we would at least be safe in our basement captivity. Not to mention Bess and George would be safe.

Adam shrugged. "That depends on how you behave," he said lightly, but he didn't meet our eyes. I had a terrible feeling that Adam didn't *know* what would ultimately happen to us. And to be the captive of an unsure person, particularly a person like Adam who was worried about what we might do when released back into the world, was bad news.

Adam reached into his pocket and pulled out a handful of zip ties, the sort of thing you might use to tie off a garbage bag. The narrow strips of plastic were surprisingly strong, and I had seen them used to bind prisoners' hands. "There is a car waiting outside," he said. "You will let me tie your hands, and you will cooperate with me, because you do not want to know what will happen to you if you don't."

I glanced at Anna and nodded almost imperceptibly. At this point we had to cooperate. We had no other option.

Adam came forward to secure my hands behind my back with the zip ties, then did the same to Anna. "Now we go," he said.

Taking us each roughly by the arm, he led us out of the storage room, down the fluorescent-lit hall, and up a set of stairs to an outside door.

The sunshine was dazzlingly bright, and I squinted my eyes, which had been surrounded by darkness for too long. I craned my neck, greedily trying to take in all the information I could, but all I observed before I was shoved toward the car was that we were near a large, industrial building, and the daylight suggested that it was mid-to late afternoon.

The car was a nondescript black town car, and as we approached, the driver exited the vehicle and opened the back door. He glanced at us quickly, not meeting our eyes. I wondered just what he knew.

I hesitated as Adam pushed us toward the car. All of the experts say to never get into a car with a captor. Once you're in the car, they can take you anywhere, do anything to you. But what choice did Anna and I have? We were not only protecting our safety by playing along, but the safety of Bess and George . . .

Suddenly the quiet afternoon was shattered by a loud, distorted voice. "*Smile!*" it screamed, so loudly amplified that I couldn't tell where it was coming from. "*You're on camera!*"

CAB CHASE

"What the—" Adam dropped my arm and Anna's as he craned his neck to find the source of the voice. "Who's there?!"

I was craning my neck too. With one quick look behind me, I found them: Bess and George! Bess was shouting into a voice distorter, probably the same one Piper had used a few days earlier to stage a protest falsely accusing Pretty Face of cruelty to animals. And George was, indeed, filming the whole scene with a tiny digital camcorder.

Waves of relief crashed over me. I don't think I had ever been so happy to see my friends.

I didn't have much time to bask in the news,

though. Right after I spotted them, Adam whipped around and lurched after Bess and George. "You there!" he cried. "Put the camera down or you'll regret it!"

George was already backing away, still filming Adam's approach with the camcorder. "Nancy! *Run!*" Bess screamed into the voice distorter, right before she and George made a break for it themselves. I glanced at Anna. "We should split up," I instructed quickly, already moving to run off to my left. "We'll be harder to catch!"

Anna nodded, and we were off.

With no time to figure out where Bess and George had headed, I just picked a random direction and started running as fast as I could. It was hard to keep my balance with my hands still bound behind my back, but I did the best I could. We seemed to be in a small industrial park bordering the water. Since I couldn't see land on the other side, I assumed we were actually looking at the ocean, and not the Hudson or East Rivers.

I ran until I could barely breathe—around buildings, across driveways, down alleys. In front of an older-looking factory I found an old-fashioned boot scraper, a piece of metal that workers in the old days would use to literally scrape the dirt off their boots. Leaning down, I managed to hook a piece of my plastic bindings over its edge, then pulled up with all of my might. The force of the breaking plastic knocked me over, but my hands were finally free.

Getting back to my feet, I took a left, and realized that the whole industrial area bordered on a small neighborhood of shops and apartments. I ran across the street and kept running—up, down, around buildings—any place I could find. Finally I paused in the middle of a crowded boulevard, looking around for any sign of Bess, George, Anna, or—gulp—Adam. Amazingly, I didn't see any of them. As I turned toward the direction I was headed, trying to figure out what to do next, a sign on a storefront just to my left caught my attention: HYUNGKOO'S LIVE POULTRY. In spite of my panic, I smiled. That explained the chicken noises—and the source of the Wi-Fi connection I'd picked up.

But then I made a scary realization: If I could hear the chickens from the basement we'd been held in, that meant I must be very close to where I started. I must have run in a huge circle. And that meant that Adam must be close by . . .

"Hey!"

A car screeched to a halt next to me. Instinctively I cowered, but then the rational part of my brain recognized the voice as George's. Flooded with relief, I looked up just in time to see George's arm reaching out to grab me and pull me into the cab.

"Oof!" I cried as my knees hit the backseat.

"Come on, Nance," Bess said impatiently, reaching over to help me in and nodding to the driver to keep going. "We don't have a ton of time. We just passed Adam, and he was headed back to his car!"

George slammed the door behind me, and the cab started moving. Sprawled across my two friends in the backseat, I struggled to get up and get my bearings. "How . . . where . . . ?"

"We're in Queens," Bess supplied, instinctively understanding my confusion. "Waaay out near JFK Airport; practically on Long Island."

"We got here just in time," George added, leaning over to squeeze my arm. "Sheesh, Nance, we were so worried! Just a few seconds later, we would have missed you, and you'd be on your way who-knows-where with that creepy guy. Good thing you were still in the city! If we'd had to go any farther, we wouldn't have found you in time."

I looked around, trying to make sense of all this. "How did you *find* me?"

George shrugged. "I plugged *Hyung Koo* and *New York* into a search engine." She explained. "Hyung Koo's Live Poultry at 43 Belleview Boulevard was the first thing to pop up. I remembered what you'd said about the chickens, and I knew it was the right place."

"So we grabbed a cab," Bess continued. "We went to Hyung Koo's, and then we just kind of searched the area. We spotted that industrial park on the water, and there was something called PFD Research Laboratories. We decided to check it out, and that's when we spotted you and Anna being led to the car."

I laughed, amazed at my friends' resourcefulness. "And the voice distorter?"

George and Bess looked at each other sheepishly, and George laughed. "We borrowed it from Piper," she admitted. "We didn't have a real plan for saving you, but we figured it might be a good distraction tactic."

I shook my head. "For not having a plan, you did pretty well."

Bess grinned. "Anytime, Nancy."

Suddenly I remembered what Adam had said. "Did anybody . . . threaten you?" I asked. "Chase after you, frighten you?"

George looked surprised. "No. Why would they?"

I sighed. "Anna told me when she regained consciousness that the phone I used to call you was bugged. Pretty Face immediately knew that we were conscious, that we had a phone, and that I had called you."

Bess shrugged. "I guess we got out of the hotel before they could find us," she said. "We climbed into this cab, and by then we must have been pretty much untraceable."

I sighed again, with relief this time. We were driving out of the residential section, getting to the wide street that separated the waterfront industrial park from the rest of the neighborhood. Suddenly it occurred to me that I hadn't seen Anna since I left the industrial park—and that the last time I'd seen her, her hands had been bound. Had she been caught? Was she alone? Frightened?

I knew I couldn't leave her here, all alone—or worse, with Adam.

"Guys," I said, "we have to find Anna."

Bess frowned. "We've been trying," she said. "No trace of her. I'm afraid . . ."

But just then, as if she'd read my mind, I

spotted her. She was running out of the industrial park, and it looked as though she'd found a way to free her hands.

She looked terrified! She ran, panting, into the street, but had to stop as a car raced by her. And then I saw who was behind her. Adam. He was hot on her heels, only about twenty feet behind her, if that. Anna looked desperately into the street as more cars sped by.

"There she is!" I cried. "And Adam's right behind her. We have to get her!"

"Stop the cab!" Bess cried, leaning over to address the driver. "Right here. If we can just get her attention . . ."

But George was way ahead of her. "ANNA!" she screamed, opening the door and waving furiously. "ANNA! OVER HERE!"

Anna turned and spotted George, her face flooding with relief. But just as she saw us, so did Adam. And his expression was murderous. Anna started running toward our cab, but Adam was gaining on her. . . .

By the time Anna reached the cab, Adam was just a couple of feet away. George leaned out of the cab and grabbed Anna's arms, pulling her into the car and sending her sprawling across the backseat, the same way she'd done with me.

Adam reached after her, and his arm was inside the taxi, blocking us from closing the door. His eyes were dark and cold, and he looked furious, ready to do almost anything to keep us from leaving him behind.

"You were so close," he chided in a low, serpentine voice. "You could have left without her. But now you'll all suffer. . . ."

All three of us were clawing at his arm, trying to push it—and him—out and away from the door, so we could close it and get away. Our cab driver saw what was going on, too, and had turned to watch the action.

"Only four people in a cab!" he yelled, leaning back to push Adam's hand out. "You get your own cab!"

Between the four of us pushing Adam, and Anna kicking at him with her feet, we had almost managed to push him out of the car. My heart was pounding in my ears, my whole body filled with adrenalin. If Adam got in, if we didn't get away from him, then this cab driver wasn't going to be able to save us from whatever fate Adam had in mind.

"Start driving!" Bess begged as she pushed mightily and got Adam's arm out of the backseat.

"Not with the door open!" the cabbie insisted.

Adam managed to grab onto the door frame, his fingers clawing desperately at the side of the door. "You won't get away . . . ," he threatened. But just then, Anna righted herself on the back-seat and lunged toward Adam's hand with her head. In one quick motion she opened her mouth and bit down *hard* on Adam's clinging fingers.

"Owwwwwwww!" He howled.

But we didn't hear any more. Bess took advantage of his momentary weakness and shoved him hard, sending him sprawling onto the pavement. I reached after her, grabbed the door, and slammed it shut, locking it securely.

"Okay," Anna addressed the driver, sounding surprisingly put together as she wiped her mouth and sat upright in the seat. "We're going to the Horatio Hotel in Manhattan, please."

The driver pounded the gas, and we were off.

TRAIN TRACKS

"**H**e's watching us," Bess complained, keeping an eye on Adam Bedrossian as he grew smaller and smaller in the rearview window. "He's writing something down. . . ."

"The medallion number," Anna said with a sigh, putting her head in her hands and moaning. "Ugh. This isn't over, guys."

"What does that mean?" I asked. "What does it mean if he has our medallion number?"

Anna pointed to a video screen that was nested onto the back of the cab's front seat, facing us. "See that?" she asked.

We glanced at the video. It was playing a touristy little intro to New York City—Visit the

Empire State Building! See a Broadway show!

"Yeah," George said slowly.

Anna rubbed her eyes, looking tired. "They were installed in almost all New York City cabs a while back. The cabs have those kinds of video screens. The screen makes it possible to pay by credit card, and"—she sighed—"it also has GPS."

It hit George first. "So anyone could tell where we are right now?"

Anna shook her head. "That's one good thing. Only the police and cab companies have access to the GPS information. But if Pretty Face has friends among the police . . ."

"Which is totally possible . . . ," I supplied, remembering what Adam had told us in the research facility.

"Then we could be in trouble," Anna finished.

We were quiet for a minute or two. The cab was flying down a main boulevard, fast enough to send us lurching forward every time he reluctantly hit the brakes. I didn't know what to do. Stay in the cab, and there was a small but decent chance Adam would find us. Or get out of the cab in a completely unfamiliar neighborhood, not knowing if there was a subway nearby, and with the potential for Adam to still find us by poking around wherever the cabbie let us out.

We stopped at a red light at a four-way intersection. "Uh-oh," Bess murmured, looking to the left. "Well, there's that question answered."

It was a black town car. Apparently Adam's town car—I trusted that Bess knew cars well enough to recognize it even after one brief sighting.

"Guys . . . ," said Bess nervously.

Anna leaned toward the driver just as the light turned green. "Punch the gas!" she cried. "Please! Sir, there's an extra fifty dollars in it for you if you can keep us away from that black car."

The cabbie looked nonplussed. "What do you girls think this is?" he asked, easing his foot off the brake for the first time in the entire ride and slowly, safely, pulling across the intersection. "The movies?"

Just then the black car screeched into action. Running the red light, it darted into traffic, causing a cacophony of honks and beeps as cars screeched out of its way. It was aimed right at us.

"Sir, please!" Anna pleaded. "This is an emergency!"

The cabbie relented and then hit the gas, hard, and we barreled down the boulevard. Adam's car stayed behind us, unable to keep up but never more than a few feet behind. The cabbie was watching him the whole time in the rearview mirrors.

"What are you girls involved in?" he asked, braking quickly to avoid a bike messenger and then barreling into the lane next to him. "I don't want any trouble. I want you out of my cab!"

"Please, sir," Anna pleaded again, turning around to look back and forth between the cabbie and Adam's driver. "Please! Just get us out of this safely."

The chase went on for too many blocks to count, our cabbie complaining bitterly the whole time and threatening to leave us on the next curb but never doing it. Horns honked, brakes screeched, and more than once we missed a full collision by inches. Bess, George, Anna, and I sat in a silent trance, too frightened to open our mouths to disturb the temporary bubble of safety we'd wandered into.

Finally, at a traffic light, we pulled away just as it turned from yellow to red. Adam's driver punched the gas behind us, but suddenly there was a huge *boom* as a truck advanced and cut them off! We heard the screech of the town car's brakes, and while the truck still blocked Adam's view, Anna convinced our cabbie to turn down a side street and make a confusing series of turns that would (hopefully) leave Adam dumbfounded.

"Oh my gosh," Bess said breathlessly, sitting up in her seat. "Oh my gosh. Do you think we could have lost him?"

Anna's expression was still steely. "Only for a few minutes," she insisted, telling the cabbie to pull over at the next intersection. "We have to get out here. Once Adam places his call to whoever and finds the cab with the GPS, he'll be right on us again."

I looked around. "Get out? Here?" I asked. We were in what looked like a quiet neighborhood with old, brick apartment buildings and the occasional Laundromat. Where would we even hide? "Do you know where we are?"

Anna didn't answer me, pressing a wad of bills into the cabbie's hand as the meter clicked and printed out a receipt. I could tell she was paying way more than the metered fare. "Let's go," she said, and we opened the door and slipped out. "Follow me."

Bess and George and I got out, following Anna down the street, into a driveway, around a building, down an alley. I tried to stay quiet for as long as possible, but as we cut across the third backyard, I had to say it. "Do you know where we're going?" I asked Anna.

But Anna didn't respond. She was already focused on something, looking upward, her eyes focused on a point halfway up in the sky. I turned to follow her gaze and saw it: an elevated train. The subway.

"Come on," she said briskly, cutting down another driveway and to the street, turning toward the train station. "We don't have much time before he finds us."

The four of us ran up the seemingly endless flights of steps to reach the station's turnstiles, then up two more flights to the platform. We were at a stop on the 7 train, in a neighborhood that Anna told us was called Jackson Heights. "A friend of mine used to live here," she explained, her eyes glued to the spot on the horizon where the train would appear. "I recognized a restaurant we used to eat at back on the main boulevard. I've spent a lot of time on this platform."

In the middle of a lazy summer afternoon—for everyone else, at least—there were only a few other people waiting for a train. The air was strangely silent, with only the occasional noise of a car or the bark of a nearby dog. I looked at

Bess and George; they looked as shell-shocked as I felt.

"Where are we going?" Bess asked finally. "Back to the hotel?"

I glanced at Anna, who shrugged, and nodded. "I guess so," I replied. "I don't feel safe in this neighborhood; Adam knows we're here. If we go back to Manhattan, we can put our evidence together and go right to the police. Maybe I can even call my dad before we go . . . In case Pretty Face does have connections to the NYPD."

"And our evidence consists of . . . ," Anna prompted.

"This." George held up the tiny video camera, clicking a button so that it showed Adam leading Anna and I, hands still bound behind our backs, out of the research building and toward the car. "Obviously he's holding you guys against your will. That's enough to get him arrested."

Bess nodded. "And as for everything else . . ." She paused. "What *is* everything else, Nance? What did you guys find out?"

I gulped, looking around at our fellow platform hangers. I didn't know why I felt so unsafe in this area; any minute now, I expected to see Adam come running up the stairs to the platform. "It's pretty much what I was afraid of," I replied. "Perfect Face contains a frog toxin that may cause paralysis after continued use. Kyle and Adam know about it, and even though Anna recommended a ten-year study to really learn of the long-term effects, they still want to rush the product to market before any competitors beat them to it."

George nodded solemnly, looking at Anna. "And you were the one who found out about the toxin in the first place?"

Anna nodded. "Yes. The frog is from Venezuela, and I remembered the indigenous people using it, but never for extended times. I found an article that suggested the ten-year study and brought it to Kyle's attention. When they ignored me for a year, I decided to go to the press." She frowned. "Big mistake. They found out somehow. And here we are."

"Wow," whispered Bess, touching her face. "Oh my gosh. That's why Perfect Face feels so tingly!" She gulped. She looked devastated. I knew Bess had really loved the Perfect Face revitalizer, and had taken to wearing it every day since we got to New York.

"I'm sure you're fine, Bess," I put in. "You've only been using it for a few weeks. Anna is talking about the damage caused from using it for years."

"Still." Bess scrunched up her nose, then started making crazy expressions by moving her eyebrows, her cheekbones, her jaw. I realized she was trying to make sure she still had use of all her facial muscles. "I'll never trust a cosmetics company again!"

Anna sighed and returned her gaze to the horizon. She was looking impatient now; fidgeting with her hands, shifting her weight from foot to foot.

"Are you okay?" I asked.

Anna shook her head. "I just don't know where this train is," she replied tersely. I met her eyes and realized that she was terrified. "It's just, we've been here for almost ten minutes," she went on, looking up and down the tracks. "If Adam does have access to the cab's GPS, he knows where he let us out, and he probably knows this is the nearest subway station. . . ."

I gulped, looking back over to the staircase. "You think he could be coming?"

Anna shrugged. "It's likely."

We were standing in the middle of the station, about ten feet from where the overhang ended and a chest-high wall separated the platform from the busy street below. I walked over to the wall, took a deep breath, and looked down at the street. A lone old woman exited a bodega with a small shopping cart, and a shaggy dog stood in a small yard behind a wire fence, barking at her. I craned my head to the left and then to the right, but they were the only signs of life on the street.

I breathed a sigh of relief. But wait: I couldn't see the station entrance below us. He could be running up the stairs to the turnstiles right now. Or just steps away from the platform . . .

My heart was beginning to speed up, thumping rapidly. I was beginning to realize the danger of our situation. If the train came and we could get on it without Adam seeing us, we were golden. We could safely ride back to Manhattan and breathe a sigh of relief. But if the train didn't come soon, we didn't have many options. We could run down the stairs, not knowing whether we might meet Adam on the way down or at the bottom, but then where could we go?

We were standing on a platform fifty feet above the city. Trapped.

I walked back to my friends. George looked at me with concern, and I could see that she was picking up on how tense Anna and I were. "Should we leave?" she asked nervously.

Anna shook her head. "Staying here is our

best option," she replied. "If the train comes before he does, we'll be safe. If we leave, we don't know what we're running into, and he could still find us."

Bess frowned. "How often do the trains usually come?" she asked.

Anna sighed. "Every ten minutes or so," she replied. "But service can be a little slow on weekends."

I followed her gaze toward the horizon, staring; willing a train to appear. Then I ran back to the wall. No one below now; even the dog had gone inside. But was Adam down there, directly below me? Was he starting up the steps right—

"Oh my gosh," Bess cried, and I saw that she had run over to the wall on the opposite side of the platform shelter. "Oh my gosh. Look!"

The three of us ran over to Bess and followed her pointing finger with our eyes. There he was, down a side street below: Adam Bedrossian, in his dark suit, running toward the train station.

"Oh no," I cried breathlessly. "What do we do now?"

Anna shook her head. I could tell she didn't know. Two staircases led down from our platform, and if we tried to run back to the street, we'd be running right into Adam. I followed Anna's gaze to the outbound platform opposite ours. It had a separate stairway, but it was separated from us by two sets of tracks and several scary-looking electrical boxes, all set on wooden slats that didn't look like they were made to be traversed.

I glanced at Anna and shook my head slightly, but I could see the panic in her eyes. What else could we do?

Just then I heard a rumble. I looked and was nearly blinded by the glint of the sun off the approaching, bright silver 7 train.

"No way," whispered George.

"Thank goodness!" Bess cried.

"Just hope it picks up quickly," Anna said, still looking tense. The train rattled into the station, and it seemed to take forever for the doors to open. Looking inside, I could now see that the train was packed with passengers; we'd be able to get on, but we'd have to stand.

As soon as the doors opened, we barreled our way into a car in the center of the train. Grabbing a spot near the middle of the car, we stared at the doors, willing Adam not to enter. After a few minutes, a chime sounded—*bing bong*—and the doors closed. But they immediately bounced back open as though they had hit something.

Bing bong. Bing bong. The doors kept opening

and closing. I thought my heart would burst out of my chest.

An announcement came over the PA, but it was so garbled, I had no idea what it was. It sounded angry.

"Someone's holding the doors open," Anna explained tensely.

Finally, after what seemed like an eternity, the doors shut and didn't open again. The silence, after all the bing bonging, felt strange. I looked at Bess and George, and the three of us heaved huge sighs of relief. We could feel the brakes release, and grabbed onto something as the train slowly pulled out of the station.

"Wow," Bess said, shaking her head. "I've never felt so happy to make a train."

Just then, there was horrible sound—the screech of metal against metal. I turned and saw that someone was walking through the door that separated our car from the next one.

My heart seized.

It was Adam.

PASSWORD PUZZLE

Anna saw him at the same time I did. She grabbed George, Bess, and me, and started barreling for the door on *our* side of the car. Adam was quickly advancing on us, but the crowds in the car weren't helping his case. We tried to move as fast as we could, and we definitely made a few enemies along the way, briskly pushing between clumps of people and pushing backpacks and strollers out of our path.

Finally Anna grabbed the metal handle of the door and slid it open along its metal track. It made another screeching sound, and then the car was filled with the noise of the train racing over the elevated tracks. Anna moved forward; a tiny

platform on the end of our car met a tiny platform of the next one, and the two compartments
were connected by a flimsy-looking chain rail-
ing. The cars were bouncing over the tracks, the
platforms never completely connecting.

I looked down and gulped: big mistake. We
were on a small platform on a moving train at
least fifty feet above the street. I felt my knees
turn rubbery.

Screech! Anna quickly crossed over to the other
platform, opened the door to the next car, and
darted inside. "Come on!"

I swallowed, trying not to think it over too
deeply, and followed her. Bess and George followed too, and within seconds we were inside the
next car, being stared at by a group of bemused
tourists. Anna kept moving forward, pushing
through toward the door at the opposite side of
the train. I glanced behind us and shivered: Adam
was right there, opening the door we'd just used.
I clambered after Anna.

We kept going, running from car to car until
I lost track of which one we were in. We caused
a little commotion in each car, pushing through
from end to end and with Adam never more than
a full car length behind. I knew we were in trouble: the subway trains only had eight or ten cars,

and sooner or later we would reach the last car and have nowhere to go.

What could Adam do to us in this crowded subway train? I didn't know, but somehow all these people didn't make me feel any safer. I knew one thing: If Adam could force us off the train with him, he could do anything he wanted.

We ran through another doorway. I'd almost gotten used to passing between cars now; we were even getting good at it. The car in front of us was bright and sunny—too sunny. With a sinking feeling I realized it was because we had finally arrived at the last car; sunlight streamed in through the opposite window.

We were trapped. And Adam was right on our heels!

In the middle of the car, a team of teenagers was performing a break-dancing routine. It was amazing, really, that they could even keep their balance on the swaying, swerving train—never mind land jumps and flips and other maneuvers. When we ran into the car and started barreling through, looking scared and all business, the team paused its performance. The car full of spectators followed the performers' gaze to us, looking puzzled.

The lead dancer, a young guy wearing a black

T-shirt and low-slung jeans, met Anna's eyes. Wordlessly he moved aside, music from their boom box still blasting, and his fellow dancers followed suit. We passed them, Anna in the lead, and walked to the end of the train. But there was nowhere to go. We paused by the last set of doors, looking out at the tracks with despair.

"How close are we to the next station?" Bess asked Anna.

"Close," Anna replied, looking grim, "but not close enough."

Just then the music was interrupted by the screech of metal on metal, and suddenly Adam appeared at the far end of the car, a murderous look in his eyes. He spotted us, trapped at the end of the train, and a tiny smirk of victory played on his face. He began walking toward us. Instinctively I cowered against the door, but there was no way to disappear.

The breakdancers had resumed their performance. Adam stalked briskly toward them, stepping on toes and pushing people aside along the way. When he was in front of the dancers, he reached out to push the head dancer out of the way, but the teenager stopped and grabbed Adam's arm.

"Watch it," he warned, twisting Adam's arm

into a lock and forcing him to look him in the eye. "What can I do for you, man?"

Adam glared, trying—and failing—to yank his arm away. "Let go of me," he cautioned.

The dancer just frowned. "It looks to me like those girls don't want to talk to you," he said simply.

Adam looked at the guy, dark intentions playing in his eyes. "It doesn't matter what they want," he replied. "That's my daughter and her friends. They're misbehaving, and I need to get to them."

The dancer shook his head. "I dunno," he said, holding tighter to Adam's arm and blocking his path with his body. "They look pretty grown-up to me. And you're awful young to have a daughter that age."

Just then the train's brakes began to screech, and I could see that we were pulling into a station. Relief flooded my chest. But would the dancer detain Adam long enough for us to get off the train?

Adam yanked on his arm, but the kid was holding on to him tightly. "I'm warning you to let me go!" he insisted. "You have no right! They'll get off here and I'll lose them!"

But the dancer's mouth was set in a grim line.

"I'm okay with that," he replied. "In fact, buddy, something about you makes me feel like it's *much better* that those girls get away from you, than I would feel about having you catching up with them."

A wave of gratitude washed over me. The train slowed and slowed and slowed some more, until I began to wonder whether we would ever stop. Finally, though, we did. *Bing, bong.* The doors slid open, and for a moment, I was so engrossed in watching the dancer hold Adam off that Anna had to shove me out the train.

"Come *on*, girls!" she yelled, running madly for the stairs. "Let's go! Run like your lives depend on it!"

We did. I was dying to look back to see if Adam was able to get off the train, but I didn't dare. We couldn't afford the seconds it would cost us. We flew down the stairs, through the turnstiles, and out of the station. Below, on a quiet residential street, Anna led the way down side streets, through alleys, across a baseball field, until we broke down and doubled over, all of us panting and wheezing. Anna gasped for air as she searched the perimeters of the field.

"No . . . sign . . . of him," she panted.

We were silent for a few minutes, all of us

struggling to regain our breath and our composure.

"That guy really saved us," Bess wheezed after a while.

George nodded. "Seriously," she agreed. "That was awesome!"

"Don't ever let anyone tell you all New Yorkers are mean," Anna replied, looking over the streets that bordered the field. "I think he knew something fishy was going on. And he wasn't just going to sit back and let it happen."

Bess followed Anna's gaze around the park, biting her lip. "So . . . ," she said, "what do we do now?"

George, Anna, and I all groaned at the same time, considering our limited options.

"Well," I said. "We're being pursued by a violent clean-up guy with no morals, we're in a strange city—except for you, Anna—and if I'm right about just how much Pretty Face wants us to go away, I'd bet the whole company is looking for us now, along with the pageant officials." I paused.

"You can count on that," Anna agreed. "Adam isn't the only bad guy in the Pretty Face corporation, believe me."

"Maybe we should just go to the police," Bess suggested with a shrug. "I'm sure there must be a precinct nearby. The camcorder footage George has alone—"

Suddenly George groaned. "Oh *crap*," she cried.

We all turned to her. "George?" I prompted.

In response, George just held up her empty hands.

"Oh *nooooo* . . ." Bess moaned.

"I must have dropped it on the train," George said.

I glanced at Anna. She still had on her game face, but I could tell she was disappointed. "Well," she said quietly. "That makes things a little more complicated."

"It means we have no evidence," I agreed, trying furiously to think of a solution. "We could still go to the police for protection. But they'd probably think we're out of our minds."

"Or worse," Anna said. "Guys, Pretty Face is *really* serious about keeping us quiet and getting this product on the market. Adam might have been telling the truth when he threatened Nancy and me back at the research facility. . . . They really might have someone inside the NYPD."

Bess gulped. "Well, what are the chances of that?"

Anna shook her head. "I wouldn't put anything

past Pretty Face or Adam Bedrossian."

We were silent for a few minutes, each thinking our separate thoughts. My mind was racing. We were in huge danger here. Who knew? Adam could have managed to get off the train, and was running toward us right this second! We needed some way to find safety. Evidence of Pretty Face's wrongdoing would keep us from immediate harm. If we could just show the police *something* . . .

That's when it hit me. "Robin!" I cried, looking at Anna. She looked back at me like I was crazy, and Bess and George looked like they agreed.

"Robin *Depken*?" said Bess.

I nodded. "Anna told me that she and Robin were in contact last year, after the pageant. Anna confided in her about the toxin problem, and Robin eventually used an e-mail she sent to try to blackmail her way into the Miss Pretty Face crown."

Bess's jaw dropped. "So . . ."

"That's why she was disqualified," I explained, "and that was around the same time Portia was dethroned, primarily because she asked too many questions."

George was looking from me to Anna, and suddenly recognition flashed in her eyes. "E-mail!" she cried. "If we could just get a printout . . ."

Anna was already shaking her head sadly. "They wiped my hard drive, guys," she said. "I put all my evidence on a flash drive that I gave to Robin. But we don't even know if she's trust-worthy. . . .

Bess frowned, glancing at me. "We don't?"

"Anna was kidnapped by Pretty Face right after giving Robin the evidence," I explained. "It could be coincidence. But—"

"Listen to me," George broke in, address-ing Anna. "Do you remember Robin's e-mail address?"

"Sure," Anna said slowly, not understanding. "It was redrobin@quickmail.net."

"Fastmail." George's face broke into a grin. "Perfect. That's Web based. We could access it from any computer."

"Do you know her password?" Anna asked, looking skeptical.

"No, but I could give it a good guess." George smirked, glancing from Anna to Bess to me. "This is my chance to make up for losing the cam-corder! Get me to a computer, guys, and I'll get you your evidence."

● ● ●

Suds, Bytes & Beans was a little hole-in-the wall storefront that seemed to be a little bit of everything: a Laundromat/Internet café/espresso bar. It took us only ten minutes to find it, wandering the streets around the baseball field until we came to what looked like the main drag.

"Uh-oh," Anna said lightly, pointing to a photo of a cappuccino in the window as we walked through the door. "This neighborhood is officially gentrifying. Prepare for rents to go up."

Bess looked confused. "What?"

Anna shrugged. "Never mind. It's a New York thing."

Inside, a lone older woman flipped through a *Good Housekeeping* magazine as her laundry spun endlessly in the dryer. A man stood behind the espresso-bar/change station, looking up only briefly from a TV mounted on the wall as we came in.

"Do you have Internet service?" George asked.

The man pointed to an ancient-looking computer in the corner and turned back to the TV. "Five dollars an hour."

"You got it." George pulled a five out of her wallet, slapped it on the counter, and we all followed her to the dark corner where the computer hummed comfortingly. George sat down and jiggled the mouse. "Wow," she murmured with a grin as the screen came to life. "Windows *ninety-eight.* Gotta admire their loyalty."

Bess looked at her blankly. "Are you on the Internet yet?"

George clicked the mouse and smiled. "I am now." She typed something into the navigation bar, and up came a cheerful blue screen with a logo for Fastmail—"When you just can't wait to connect." She clicked on the Login icon and typed *redrobin* into the username field.

"Does Robin have a boyfriend?" George asked Anna.

Anna nodded. "She used to," she replied. "A guy named Derek Kizer."

George typed *derekkizer* into the password field, and when that didn't work, *Derek, cutederek, iloved-erek,* and *robinkizer.* Nothing worked. "Hmmm," she said. "Robin's a tougher nut to crack than I thought."

"Try *River Heights University,*" I suggested. "Or *RHU.*"

George tried both; neither was the password.

"How about *Piper*?" asked Beth. "That's her sister. Or maybe she has a crush on a celebrity. . . ."

George was typing furiously, trying password after password and clicking the mouse as soon as possible after each attempt. Each time, the password came back wrong.

"Shouldn't it time out eventually?" asked Anna. "On my mail program, if you enter three wrong passwords, you have to wait twenty minutes and try again. It's to prevent people from breaking into your account."

George nodded grimly. "Let's just say Fastmail isn't known for their great security," she replied. "They're known for being free and having a cute design."

George's fingers flew over the keyboard as she listed possible passwords: *New York Yankees. Boston Red Sox. Chicago Cubs. Chicago White Sox* . . . She sighed. "Okay, Robin's not a big sports fan. What else, guys? What should I try?"

"You tried *password*?" Bess suggested.

George quickly typed that in. Nothing.

I sighed. "I feel like we're missing something," I explained. "Something right in front of us."

Bess looked up at the ceiling, deep in thought, and then smiled. "How about *Pretty Face*?" she asked. "Have we tried that? Or *Miss Pretty Face*?"

George shook her head, like she couldn't believe we'd missed those, and quickly typed. "Miss Pretty Face," she read, and clicked the Login button. The computer paused to load, and then slowly but surely, the brightly colored page that held Robin's in-box popped up. "I'm in."

"Wow," Anna remarked, stooping to look over George's shoulder. "A year later, and she still has *Miss Pretty Face* as her password?"

"That may be a window into her motivations," I suggested. "If she's still thinking about being Miss Pretty Face a year later . . . That gives her more of a motive to tell the bigwigs about your plans, Anna."

George was already clicking down a row of messages. "Sent messages. Sent messages," she read, clicking the folder that would lead us to Robin's out-box. The screen came up . . . totally empty. George frowned. "Guys," she said.

"Try her in-box," Anna suggested. "Maybe someone wrote to her about the pageant and her plans here . . ."

George clicked on the in-box icon. It too came up empty.

"Weird," Bess said.

"Maybe not weird," I replied, the gears turning in my brain. "Maybe totally expected. Pretty Face wiped your hard drive, right, Anna?"

Anna nodded. "They erased everything, including all my evidence about the frog toxin that was on my flash drive."

"And if they went through your e-mail," I continued, "then they would have found Robin's e-mail address and realized she was the person you were sending evidence to. George, how hard would it be for someone to do what we did, break into Robin's account and erase the whole thing?"

George shrugged. "Not hard at all," she replied. "It's just a matter of hitting Select All and Delete. Then maybe they change the password so Robin can't get back in."

I nodded. "Miss Pretty Face," I said.

"So it's either a sign she's still bitter," Anna murmured, thinking aloud, "or it's Pretty Face themselves trying to throw us off track."

"Um," Bess said urgently, suddenly grabbing my arm and pointing behind us. I realized that Bess had tuned out of the conversation and was watching the local news station, NY1, on the TV mounted on the wall. "Guys. Look."

A smiling, shiny-haired brunette smirked into the camera as a graphic of a sparkly tiara appeared over her right shoulder. "Some not-so-pretty behavior today at a pageant to determine the fairest of them all," she announced as the screen filled with images from the Horatio Hotel. "Officials at the Miss Pretty Face pageant reported today that they suspect a pageant contestant of stealing more than ten thousand dollars worth of jewelry belonging to the pageant. Among the missing items are the tiara given to the national pageant winner, which contains one carat of diamonds, plus a jeweled scepter and a pair of sapphire earrings donated for the winner by Grand Jewelry Store."

I gulped. I knew what was coming next, and yet it still surprised me.

"Police are searching for a contestant named Nancy Drew."

And there it was: my photo. I'm in my flamingo dress, tiara, and sash from the regional pageant, smiling unsurely as I waved at the audience.

"Ms. Drew was implicated when her pageant roommate, the reigning Miss Pretty Face, Kelly McMahon, spotted the sparkling tiara peeking out from Ms. Drew's luggage this afternoon. Officials have identified the items as the missing jewelry. Ms. Drew, who may be traveling with accomplices, is still at large."

The screen flashed back to the local anchors.

"Too bad those pageants don't measure *inner* beauty," suggested the male anchor.

"I think Nancy Drew can kiss that crown good-bye," the woman agreed.

I was stunned. Obviously I hadn't stolen that jewelry; Adam must have called someone in Manhattan to set it up around the time we first escaped from him. Now we weren't just running from him, but from everyone in New York City who watched the news. I glanced over at the store owner. He stared back at me, frowned, and without a word, pulled the phone from its cradle in front of him and started dialing.

"Uh-oh," I said.

But George was way ahead of me. She stood up from the computer and, pushing us all along, got us all running out of the Laundromat-Internet café-espresso bar.

The street was still empty.

"We need a cab. We have to get to Manhattan," Anna announced, searching up and down the street. "To Robin. If she still has that flash drive, she's our only hope of getting the police to take us seriously."

"And if she doesn't?" George asked.

Anna sighed. "Then it's going to be a lot harder." She paused. "Maybe we can convince them to investigate Pretty Face, at least. It would take longer. But . . ."

"And hopefully I won't be in jail for stealing a tiara while it works itself out," I piped up.

Bess patted my shoulder. "It'll be fine, Nance," she said. "You don't even *wear* jewelry!"

We were walking down the streets, searching for a yellow cab, but there were barely any cars out today, let alone taxis in this quiet residential neighborhood.

"Maybe we should take the subway," George suggested hesitantly as we turned another corner.

Anna bit her lip. "Adam could be waiting for us at the station," she replied. "That's the last place he saw us. He knows we can't stay in this neighborhood forever."

Suddenly her eyes lit up. She smiled, and then started running for a black town car that was parked in front of a grocery store.

"Anna!" I called. "That looks like some rich guy's limo!"

But Anna was shaking her head. "It's called car service, Nancy," she said, moving closer. "Or a gypsy cab. Technically you're supposed to call ahead, and they're not supposed to pick up passengers on the street. But they're a lot more common in the outer boroughs, like this, where you don't see many yellow cabs."

She walked around to the driver's window and knocked.

I sighed. "Are you sure this is safe?" I asked. I believed that Anna knew what she was talking about, but flagging down a big black car and asking for a ride still felt strange.

Anna nodded. "It's totally safe, Nancy. I take them all the time when I'm headed into the city for a night out."

There was a little buzzing sound, and the darkened window descended a few inches, revealing a middle-aged, mustached driver. "You need a ride?"

Anna nodded. "How much to Manhattan?"

The driver smiled. "Twenty dollars."

Anna sighed in relief. She looked back at us. "I have that, guys. We're saved. Let's get in."

The driver pushed a button. "I'll unlock the doors."

Anna grabbed the handle of the back door, and she was the first to pile in to the dark, leather-seated interior. Bess followed her, then George, then myself. I breathed a sigh of relief as my butt hit the soft cushioned bench. It felt so good to sit down, to be headed somewhere, out of danger, back to Manhattan and the watchful eye of thousands of people.

I slammed the door behind us, and the lock

clicked. I looked around, my eyes adjusting to the light.

"Hello, girls."

And then I saw him. Kyle McMahon, on the seat facing us.

7

A MAN WITHOUT A PLAN

Anna looked furious. "How did you find us?" she demanded.

Kyle smiled. "I've been in constant touch with Adam ever since you used Anna's phone to call your little friends, Nancy. When Adam told me that he'd lost you in this neighborhood, I had my driver take me out here so we could circle the streets for a bit. I knew you'd have to turn up eventually. And here you are."

I glared at him. "You created the story that I had stolen that jewelry, and planted the crown in my room."

Kyle nodded. "We couldn't take any chances,

could we? We didn't want you girls heading to the police. And Kelly played her part very well. She noticed the jewelry we'd planted in your luggage right away, though she was pretty torn up about turning you in. Kept saying it didn't seem like something you would do."

George frowned. "That's because it's something she *didn't* do."

Kyle turned to face her. "Ah, Bess and George," he said, looking over my two best friends. "If only you hadn't been so good at tracking Nancy down! You might have escaped all of this."

Bess gulped. "Where are you taking us?" she demanded.

Kyle looked us over, and a flicker of something—discomfort?—passed across his eyes. "Well, you ladies have proven to us that you can't be trusted," he said quietly. "The minute you get out of our sights, you begin to misbehave. The only solution is to keep you under our watchful eyes until the pageant is over and Perfect Face has been successfully launched," he went on.

"And then?" I prompted.

"And then," Kyle said. The flicker came back; definitely discomfort this time. "Then we'll see."

Uh-oh. If Kyle didn't have a plan for what to do with us . . . that was a bad sign.

"You'll see?" I asked. "What does that mean? You'll let us go?"

Kyle met my eyes, but he didn't respond. I saw all I needed to in his expression.

"You wouldn't hurt us," I insisted, trying to convince myself as much as him. "For something as simple as a marketing campaign? A new product launch?"

Kyle looked out the window.

"How much can that be worth?" I pressed. "A few million dollars? Is it worth turning into a criminal?"

Kyle turned back to us, eyes flashing. "It's not just a few million dollars," he corrected. "It's not *greed*. I'm not doing this for *greed*."

"What are you doing it for, then?" George demanded.

"My *daughter*!" Kyle shouted. We all jumped a little, taken aback by his outburst.

"It's not just the money," he continued. "Money can't buy happiness or love. But Kelly and I, we need this marketing campaign to work in order to keep our current lifestyle." He paused. "This isn't just a new product launch, not for Pretty Face. We've sunk too much money into developing and marketing this product. If Perfect Face doesn't take off, Pretty Face is sunk."

His face fell. "And so are Kelly and I."

"But you could get a new job!" Bess piped up encouragingly. "You're talented, you have a great résumé, I'm sure!"

Kyle shook his head. "I'll never find another job like this one. Not in River Heights. And Kelly has grown up there. . . . She shouldn't have to move."

I swallowed. "Kyle," I finally said. "You realize that George, Bess, Anna, and I—we're all someone's daughter, too." I paused. "And we haven't done anything wrong. We just found out the truth."

Kyle looked out the window again. He didn't respond. But he looked troubled.

The rest of the ride back to Manhattan was silent. I exchanged worried glances with Bess, George, and Anna, but there was nothing we could do—The doors were locked. We were in a moving prison. After about half an hour, we pulled up outside the Horatio Hotel. As crazy as it sounds, I actually felt relieved to see the place again. I knew we were returning as prisoners, but somehow I felt comforted just knowing that the other contestants would be nearby.

Kyle pulled a cell phone out of his pocket and pressed a button. "We're here," he announced curtly. After a few seconds Adam Bedrossian strolled out the front door. It was then that I noticed the TV cameras and photographers flanking the entrance. Someone must have tipped off the local media that Nancy Drew, pageant jewelry thief extraordinaire, had been found.

Kyle leaned over to open a window, and Adam stuck his head in. He grinned meanly at the four of us.

"So good to see you again, Nancy, Anna, and company," he said smoothly. "Let me explain what's going to happen here. I've explained to the hotel security that while we're very happy to have located you, we want the pageant to go on without interruption. All the girls are currently at the Waldorf-Astoria, getting ready. So rather than turn you in to the police just yet, we'll hold you in the hotel under my watchful eye until the pageant is over." He grinned again, exposing a mouthful of wolfish white teeth.

"And then what?" I asked, afraid to know the answer.

Adam glanced at Kyle, a dark uncertainty in his eyes. "Let's just take this one step at a time," he muttered as a couple of burly guys—hotel security, I assumed—came up behind him. "Girls, I want you to get out of the car in as orderly a manner as possible. Just know that I am armed, and I am *not* going to let you get away from me again."

I glanced at Anna and gulped. What was going to happen to us if we went up to that hotel room? Was it worth fighting Adam and risking angering him enough to shoot?

Actually, scratch that. There wasn't any uncertainty there. I was almost positive Adam was crazy enough to shoot.

Kyle leaned over and pressed a button, and the door locks released. Adam grasped the handle and opened the passenger-side door, which faced the hotel.

"Let's go," he said. "Nice and slow. Hands where I can see them."

Anna, who was closest to the curb, got out first. George followed, and then Bess, and then me. Even the fading sunlight seemed blinding after the darkness of the town car. I looked around, noting the few news cameras filming us, and then followed the security guards—Adam and Kyle positioned themselves behind us, bringing up the rear—into the hotel.

It was a strange experience, being led up to Kyle's room. People watched us, staring, whispering to one another. But the hotel wasn't very busy since the contestants had all gone ahead to begin rehearsals. The people left behind were just casual observers, people who had probably seen our faces on the news. *I didn't do it; I'm not a thief!* I wanted to shout at them. But really, their perceptions were the least of my worries right now.

"Thank you, gentlemen," Adam told the security guards when we reached Kyle's room, and he opened the door with his key card. "We'll take it from here. I'll keep an eye on the girls while the pageant goes on, and I'll call if I need any help. Thank you for your assistance."

The security guards made brief eye contact and nodded. Then they were gone, headed back into the elevator and downstairs.

Away from their eyes, Adam shoved us into the hotel room. "I want the four of you to line up and sit down on the bed!" he commanded. "Kyle, watch them while I get the restraints."

The four of us lined up on the bed, like Adam had specified. I looked into Kyle's eyes as he watched us impassively. Was he really okay with this? Was he really this kind of man?

"Adam," Kyle said weakly, seeming to read my mind. "Is this really necessary? Perhaps if you just stay by the door, we—"

Adam turned around and glared at Kyle.

"Don't ruin all your hard work by being weak," he chided. "You've seen these girls in action. You know what they're capable of. Do you want to take any chances?"

Kyle removed his glasses and closed his eyes, rubbing them tiredly. "They're just young girls," he murmured, almost to himself.

"They're dangerous," Adam insisted, walking over to the bed with duct tape in one hand and a roll of fishing line in the other. "You know that. They have to be controlled."

I spoke up. "Kyle," I said, trying to sound earnest, "you know we've learned our lesson now. If you need to launch Perfect Face for Kelly's sake, we'll keep quiet, I promise."

Kyle watched me, looking unsure. I could tell he wanted to believe me, but . . .

"She's lying," Adam said flatly, placing the fishing wire down on the bed and picking up a pair of scissors. "Now help me secure them."

Adam and Kyle weren't taking any chances. They used the duct tape to gag all four of us, then bound our hands behind our backs with the fishing wire. The sitting position was uncomfortable, and the fishing wire dug into the skin of my wrists. I glanced at Bess on my right; she looked as miserable as I felt. And the worst part was wondering when were we going to be freed. And if we ever were freed, what would happen to us then?

My heart thumped a sad rhythm in my chest. Was a frog toxin worth whatever punishment we were going to receive?

Once we were silenced and tied up, Kyle stepped away, looking out the window, looking anywhere, it seemed, but at us. He glanced at his watch. "I'd better get to the pageant," he said. "They'll be wondering what happened to me. You'll be okay here?"

Adam nodded. "Of course."

"Okay." Kyle looked at the four of us then, biting his lip, and then turned toward the door. "Use . . . sound judgment, Adam, please."

Adam looked not at Kyle but at the four of us. And he smiled his wolfish grin again.

Kyle continued, "We don't want to do anything that can't be . . . undone."

Adam looked at Kyle with contempt. "We've passed that point already, my friend."

I closed my eyes as ice flooded my veins. How would we ever get out of here?

Kyle swallowed and turned, addressing me directly. "Piper will be taking your place in the competition, Nancy."

I just blinked at him. Did he seriously think I cared about the pageant now?

"It's too bad." Kyle looked sincere as he opened the door to the hotel room with a shrug. "I know you don't think of yourself as a pageant queen, but I think you had a good shot."

I shook my head in disbelief as the door shut behind our only hope of being set free.

HOTEL HOSTAGES

"What do you think is going on right now?" Adam asked brightly, standing by the window of our hotel room. It had been about half an hour since Kyle left. Anna, Bess, George, and I were sitting miserably on the bed, wiggling and shifting every few seconds in a useless bid to keep our arms from falling asleep.

"It's five minutes to curtain," Adam continued. "Probably a lot of commotion backstage, everyone getting their makeup just right, trying to remember the words to their song or recited poem or inaugural address or whatever." He laughed sharply. "Perfume flowing, a cloud of hairspray settled over the room. Don't you miss it, Nancy?" He turned to me and laughed mockingly. "After all, isn't that what girls like you *really* want, to be told you're the fairest of them all?" He chuckled again.

"If you ask me," he went on, "it takes a pretty stupid person to want to compete in a pageant in the first place. You think it's really about celebrating beauty, representing the best in your generation? *No.*" He paused, looking over the four of us with an increasingly dark expression. "The Miss Pretty Face pageant is about one thing and one thing only: money. And marketing. Nobody cares what evening gown you wear or what you say you would do to bring about world peace, sweetheart. They only care that you smile, put on the products, and not ask too many questions."

I swallowed. I knew the pageant wasn't completely on the up-and-up, but it was different to hear Adam say it was a total sham out loud.

"And this year," he continued, "with Perfect Face launching . . . Well, there was less room for error than ever before." He smiled nastily at me. "Your little friend Robin Depken, she lost the title for herself when she found a suspicious e-mail and started asking too many questions. She tried to blackmail herself into the crown, but she only succeeded in getting herself disqualified. A multimillion dollar corporation isn't about to be bossed around by some half-wit beauty contestant." He grinned that wolfish grin again. "And your other friend. The difficult one, Portia Leoni. She wasn't dethroned because some jealous girl set her up, like you said. She was removed by *us*, Nancy Drew. In fact, I made the phone call to Fleur myself. Film her taking some dresses, then set her up for shoplifting. She's disgraced, and the crown is ours to give away to someone more . . . appropriate."

"Why?" I tried to ask, forgetting the duct tape over my mouth. It came out like a strangled cry—"Aigh?"

"Why?" Adam laughed at my attempt to speak. "Because she was a nuisance, plain and simple. She demanded too much, was late to events, and asked too many questions. She was only out for herself, but she was smart, like a fox, and we worried that if she learned too much about the cosmetics, she might eventually ask some questions that we wouldn't want to answer."

I thought this over. I'd known from Anna that no one had dethroned Portia; she had dethroned herself by being a nuisance. But Adam's take on it, that it all had to do with shutting up and marketing the brand, was interesting. Oddly enough,

Fallon—the contestant I'd accused of setting Portia up because I thought she was angry Portia had blackmailed her the year before—would have made a great Miss Pretty Face, for those concerns. She didn't care about anything except getting that crown on her head, and being an official beauty queen.

I felt a little flower of guilt blossoming in my chest. Fallon had been nasty to me, but I hated thinking that I'd killed her dream simply by being wrong.

"And so," Adam continued, still looking at us with that creepy smile, "who would we install as the new Miss Pretty Face? Fortunately the perfect candidate was right there: Kelly McMahon. Sweet, desperate to be liked, pretty, and the daughter of one of Pretty Face's rising executives. And, just between us, the girl doesn't have much going on upstairs. She's the perfect candidate to smile, wave, wear the makeup, and do what she's told."

That was unfair. Kelly was my friend and one of the nicest people I'd encountered in my pageant experience. True, she didn't ask many questions, but did *anyone* ask as many questions as I did?

I glared at Adam.

"Oh, I'm sorry, Nancy," he said, fake concern flooding his face. "Are you upset to miss out on your chance to be Miss Pretty Face America? The prizes, as I'm sure you know, are quite valuable. But I don't really think you had much of a shot. A real Miss Pretty Face knows her place—and she knows when to leave well enough alone."

Please.

Really, Adam was obviously more of a nut than I ever thought—It wasn't worth getting upset about anything he had to say. Instead, I tried to tune him out and focus on the present. The four of us were trapped in this hotel room, guarded by this crazy bulldog of a man. If we were still here when the pageant ended and Kyle came back . . .

I didn't want to think about what would happen next.

So I just decided that I would have to believe we would get out.

Desperate, I began searching the room with my eyes. There had to be something—anything—that I could use to get us out of here. Something that could be used as a weapon against Adam, or to cut through our restraints . . .

As Adam turned on the TV and settled on the couch, I took a more careful look all around. But everything I saw was expected—and useless.

A pillow. The clock radio. A pad of paper and a pen. Could I get my hands on the pen somehow? Clasp it in my hand and somehow use it to poke Adam in the eye?

I sighed. I was grasping at straws now. Hearing my sigh, George turned to me and shot me a meaningful look. She used her shoulder to gesture to Adam; I shrugged. What could we do?

How would we ever get out of here?

Just as I was starting to despair, I spotted something.

Behind George, a round table flanked by two comfortable-looking reading chairs posed as a temporary office. Kyle's laptop computer sat there, on sleep, and a few papers and folders were scattered around. To the left of all this, almost at the edge of the table, was a small red box, emblazoned with the logo for Crostini—one of New York's hottest restaurants. (I knew this because Bess had read about it in her guidebook and had been eager to try it out—until we learned the cheapest entrée cost fifty-seven dollars.)

Matches. No doubt Kyle had gone to a business dinner at Crostini and grabbed the matchbox on the way out as a souvenir of his dinner.

I swallowed, considering. *Can I? Is it worth the risk?*

Then I cleared my throat.

"Ohhh," I moaned, closing my eyes and jiggling on the bed. "Ohhh . . . Adam?" Except it didn't sound like *Adam?* through the tape. It sounded like *Ah-uh?* But apparently the point got across, because Adam turned around.

"Don't start crying now," he warned me. "You'll use up all your tears before Kyle gets back, and then how will you plead for mercy?"

An icy prickle of fear stabbed into my chest. I moaned again—"Ohhh" and wiggled on the bed some more.

Adam frowned and stood up from the couch. "I'm not untying you," he warned me. "So if you're uncomfortable now, better get used to it."

I shook my head. "Ah-oooh," I managed. "Eeeez?"

Adam sighed. He looked to Bess, George, and Anna, as though he might find some signs of conspiracy, but they looked back at him blankly. Slowly, as if it were against his better judgment, he approached me.

He grabbed one end of the duct tape and pulled it from my mouth with one quick motion. *Owwww.* A thousand pins and needles burned around my jaw.

"What do you want?" he demanded, placing his hand on my shoulder as if to hold me down.

"Bathroom," I replied quickly, trying to sound desperate. "I can't hold it any longer! You can guard the door. . . ."

Adam looked angry. And more than that, torn. I could tell that he'd never considered this. "You can hold it," he said gruffly, but he didn't walk away.

"I can't!" I insisted. "Please, just let me go, you can guard the door, and it will be better for everybody!"

Adam sighed. I could tell my pleas were working.

"*Please,*" I pleaded. "Please, please. I promise, I won't cause any more trouble if you let me go."

Finally he nodded and roughly grabbed my arm and pulled me up. "Fine," he agreed. "But no funny business. I'll wait outside the door, and after two minutes—one hundred and twenty seconds—I'm coming in."

I nodded shakily. "Okay." Bess caught my eye as I turned to follow Adam. Her expression said, *Are you up to something?* I winked at her and headed around the bed to the bathroom.

Adam was walking ahead of me, and as he opened the bathroom door, I reached out and managed to clasp the red matchbox in my hand so it didn't show.

"Okay," he said, opening the door wide and gesturing for me to go in. "To make sure you don't lock the door, I'm going to hold it like this," he said, positioning the door just an inch or so away from the closed position. You couldn't see inside, but he held the door so that the lock mechanism couldn't engage. "Two minutes, that's all you get."

I nodded. "I understand."

"Okay."

Adam stepped aside, and I walked into the bathroom. He closed the door behind me and held it in the unlatched position. I glanced at myself in the mirror. I looked as frantic as I felt. I was sweaty, my hair was a mess, and I had a panicked look, like someone had just told me a bomb was going to go off in thirty seconds.

I could feel my heart thumping, and my hands were shaking. But I had work to do and not much time to do it in. First I found Kyle's toiletry bag, right on the vanity. I dumped it out onto a towel, trying to do it quietly enough that Adam wouldn't hear, and examined the contents. Shaving cream, hand lotion . . . *Aha!* I grabbed the nail clippers. As carefully as I could, I positioned the fishing line binding my hands between the clippers, and pressed down.

Clip. And my hands were free.

I quickly grabbed the towels from the rack— except for one—and dumped them into the bathtub, along with some extra toilet paper and a box of tissues. I carefully and quietly took down the shower curtain, then wadded it up and placed it in the tub.

I took a deep breath. My hands were shaking almost too much for me to do what I needed to do. But I somehow managed.

I picked up the matches from the vanity, carefully lit one, and then threw it into the tub.

FIRE ESCAPE

It took a few seconds for the fire to get going. Impatient, I kept grabbing at whatever could burn and using them to feed the fire. Finally the tiny flames blossomed into huge yellow-orange ones, and smoke began to fill the room. I stood and waited, praying that Adam wouldn't smell the smoke too soon.

The fire was giving off a good amount of heat, and I backed away, feeling it start to singe the ends of my hair. It was an impressive blaze now, completely filling the bathtub. With a swallow, I touched the one towel I'd kept to the blaze, and then gently rested it on the bathmat. Flames licked along the length of the towel, finally catching the bathmat and starting to climb the walls.

It was then that the door crashed open. *"What are you doing?!"* Adam screamed, pushing me out of the bathroom and running toward the flames, stopping just short of them catching his jacket. "Are you crazy?! Are you trying to get us killed?"

Just then, the smoke alarm went off.

BEEP! BEEP! BEEP! BEEP!

The sound was deafening, and when I turned from the bathroom, my friends were all cowering, trying to shield their ears from the noise. Still, Bess and George were shooting me impressed smiles. I ran over to them, quickly using the nail clippers to snip through their fishing-line restraints. Soon they were all free, stretching their arms and quickly pulling off the duct tape.

"Ouch!'

"Owww!"

"Ouch!"

"What now, Nance?" George asked me, and I nodded toward the door. Adam was still in the bathroom, and I could hear the water running as he tried to battle the flames.

Without another word we ran toward the door. I grabbed the handle and turned, but—

It wouldn't open.

"You morons!" Adam cried, staggering out of the bathroom with smoke trailing behind. "Do you know what this little stunt is going to cost you girls? Do you know what you've done?"

I scrambled for the handle, pushing and pulling. The door wouldn't budge.

Suddenly Adam reached for the back of his pants and pulled out a very shiny small gun. "I dare you," he growled, his eyes dark and cold. "Escape me. I dare you!"

Suddenly George reached up and flipped a small brass lever from one side to the other. I could hear the dead bolt give way, but I was still staring at the gun, too stunned to move.

Then several things happened at once. "*Nancy!*" yelled George, shoving a small table that stood near the entrance toward Adam with her foot. As she did that, Anna turned the handle and yanked open the door, and the four of us ran out into the hallway.

I could hear Adam shouting behind us, but we kept running. George led the way down the hallway to the stairs, where hotel personnel were already running toward Kyle's room. The hotel's fire alarm was screeching at full blast, making it impossible to hear what anyone was yelling at us as we flew by. A man wearing a shirt and tie charged down the hall, holding a fire extinguisher, and it was as I turned to watch him that I spotted Adam: He'd emerged from the room and was aiming the gun at us. "Come back *now*!" he shouted. "Or you'll be sorry!"

"Nance!" Bess shrieked, turning to realize that I'd paused, and pulled me behind her into the stairwell.

"Run!" George instructed as we began down the stairs.

We ran.

We ran down the stairs so fast that a few times my feet landed in the wrong place, and I was afraid I would go hurtling forward and tumble head-over-tail down nine flights of stairs, but somehow we all stayed upright. At the bottom of the stairs, we kept running—through the security guardless lobby (since they were mostly, no doubt, trying to quell the fire and figure out what was going on in Kyle's room) and out onto the street. We glanced at one another, and then ran down the block, where we paused for just a second to take stock.

"Where?" Bess said, simply. We all knew we didn't have much time to discuss.

"The Waldorf-Astoria," I replied. "The pageant. It'll be crawling with media and police—

and Robin Depken will be there. She's our only hope of corroborating our Perfect Face story."

Anna made a face. "I hope we can do something before they unroll their marketing campaign to teenagers."

I nodded. "Me too. But we'd better go now!"

Instead of running, Anna stepped into the street and held out her arm. Within seconds, a bright yellow taxi pulled up in front of us.

"Wow," I murmured as Anna opened the door and we all piled in. "I could use these working cases back home."

"The Waldorf-Astoria," said Anna, climbing into the front seat with the driver. "And step on it!"

I knew that the Waldorf-Astoria would be mobbed because of the pageant, but that still didn't prepare me for the chaos we encountered once we got within a couple of blocks. Traffic was at a standstill with TV vans taking up half the side street and security guards desperately trying to keep people moving into the building.

"You can let us out here," Anna told the driver, even though we were still two blocks away.

As Anna pressed money into the driver's hand, Bess, George, and I piled out onto the sidewalk.

George frowned. "Where do we go?" she asked. "How are we going to get in? Should we find a policeman?"

Bess shook her head. "The police are looking for *us*, remember?" she asked, gesturing toward me. "Us and Miss Sticky Fingers River Heights over here."

I pretended to pout. "Be that as it may," I said, "we don't have a lot of choices. We need the police if we're going to bring down Pretty Face. Period."

Anna nodded. "I agree," she said. "It may take a while to work everything out, but if we can just convince them to get Robin out of the audience . . ."

"And hope against hope that Robin's on our side," I finished, "and didn't set you up."

Anna looked regretful. "Like you said," she replied. "We don't have a lot of choices."

"All right," George said, looking impatiently up the avenue toward the hotel. "There's a policeman right there. Should we try our luck?"

I nodded. "This is it," I said.

Anna sighed and looked a little fearful. But a determined expression quickly chased away that fear. "Let's go," she said.

● ● ●

"Sorry, girls." The policeman, who we could now see was youngish with sandy hair, held out his hands to stop us before we could even get within ten feet of him. "Nobody gets into the pageant without ID or a qualifying ticket. Even if you have those, you'll have to be escorted in. The show has already started, and we don't want to disrupt the telecast."

George made a face, like she'd tasted something sour, and turned to me. "It's *televised*?" she asked.

I shrugged. I didn't know.

"It's on FUN at eight o'clock," Bess replied, and was met with blank looks. "You know, the cable network for teen girls? They have that show *Make Me a Celebrity Assistant*?"

We all stared uncomprehendingly.

Bess sighed and shook her head. "I swear," she muttered. "A bunch of pop-culture illiterates."

"*Anyway*," the policeman broke in, looking amused by our exchange. "You girls will have to move along now. Good-bye, have a nice night." His gaze resting on me, suddenly he paused and gripped his bully stick. "*Wait* a minute—"

"If you're wondering whether I'm the pageant jewelry bandit," I broke in, stepping forward, "I am. Or at least, that's what Pretty Face wants you to believe. I'm willing to turn myself in right now, if you'll do me one favor."

We were handed over to pageant security to be babysat while someone fetched Robin Depken out of the audience. We were led backstage through a complex system of hidden corridors, so we wouldn't enter the ballroom and disrupt the FUN telecast. Still, I could hear the pageant going on through the walls. The big dance number was playing, and, weirdly, as not-into-the-whole-pageant thing as I had been, my feet were itching to break into the steps. I felt a sudden pinch of regret at missing the pageant.

Just a pinch, though.

We were led to a small room that held a few chairs and a television tuned to FUN. By that time, the dance number had ended, and the girls were being called up to two microphones on opposite sides of the stage in order to introduce themselves. A familiar voice sliced through me as I laid eyes on her golden hair and sparkling violet gown.

"I'm Piper Depken!" she enthused, parting her lips to reveal her perfect Vaseline smile. "I'm representing River Heights, and I want to be a teacher when I grow up!"

A teacher? Did she really? I tried to envision the cutthroat Piper, who'd pouted about the pageant and even tried to sabotage Pretty Face with a fake protest, working with kids. Well, it was hard to know who the real Piper was these days.

Looking up, I realized two security guards had entered, and the one who had led us here was gesturing to the ballroom. "I'm going to go now," he told us. "I'll get who you need. The police are on their way in. Once she's back here, you can all sit down for a little powwow."

We all nodded. "Thanks," said Anna.

He left. We looked at one another for a few seconds, then quietly sat down on the seats provided. We were silent, the pageant playing in the background.

"This is it," said Anna finally.

"Right," I agreed. "We can only hope that you were right to trust Robin."

"If not . . ." Anna shuddered. "I hate to think of what will happen."

I swallowed. We were in police custody now, which felt safer than being in Kyle or Adam's care. But that still didn't guarantee a good outcome. If Robin didn't back up our story, then the best we could hope for was the police holding me for the ridiculous jewelry theft charge.

If they released us—Well, let's just say I was sure Adam or Kyle would find us before long.

"When I want to catch a guy's attention, I reach for my Perfect Face!"

The young, almost musical voice came from the TV, and we all turned to look. Five pageant contestants were acting out a little skit—what essentially looked like a live ad for Pretty Face.

A petite redhead took a tube of Perfect Face from a tall blonde and squirted some in her hand, rubbing it onto her face. "Perfect Face makes everyone look like a perfect ten!" she said with a giggle, then passed the tube along to another blonde.

"I love the way it tingles!" the blonde said. "But more than that, I love how it evens out my complexion."

"I never have acne when I'm wearing my Perfect Face," a curly haired brunette chimed in.

"Everyone can look perfect with Perfect Face!" The girls all moved in toward the camera, smiling and smearing the cream over their faces.

Anna and I looked at each other with disgust. The ad campaign had started already!

"Girls," a deep voice chimed from the doorway. It was the same security guard who had left earlier. We all turned around.

"I think I've brought the person you need to see."

The security guard moved aside, and someone stepped behind him into the room. Someone bigger than Robin. And taller. And male.

Kyle McMahon.

10

KEY WITNESS

Kyle regarded the four of us with a grim, if not entirely surprised, expression. "Well, well, well," he said slowly. "Thank you, Peter," he said to the guard who'd led him in. "I'm going to need your help . . . restraining these girls."

We just stood there, stunned, until Bess came to her senses and let out a scream. "AAAHH!" But no sooner had she started screaming than one of the beefy security guards grabbed her and clamped his meaty hand over her mouth. Bess made a screeching noise and tried to bite his hand, but he held firm.

Before the rest of us could react, we were

each grabbed by a different guard.

Kyle was shaking his head sadly. "You girls," he said, his voice warm with regret. "You girls. In a way, it's charming the way you trust authority. But did it ever occur to you that security guards at the Pretty Face pageant might be more loyal to Pretty Face than the local police?" He paused. "Why couldn't you just have left well enough alone? You know me, Nancy. . . ."

He turned to me. I stared back at him, slowly shaking my head. I did *not* know Kyle McMahon. If this whole pageant experience had taught me anything, it was that.

"I'm a family man," Kyle continued. "I have nothing against you girls as people. I'm sure you're all lovely, bright young women." His expression darkened, and he lowered his voice. "But I cannot—*cannot*—have you interfering in Pretty Face's affairs. The success of Perfect Face is simply too important—to the company and to me, personally."

"But you've lost sight of what really matters! You're willing to hurt us—maybe even kill us—all for the sake of money and success!" That's what I tried to yell around the hand of my burly restrainer. What actually came out was, "Brrrrrrrt urrrrrr maaa! Essss!" Still, I guess my outburst was enough to engage Kyle's attention. He looked curiously at me, then at my guard.

"Let her speak," he commanded. "Nancy, if you scream or try to draw attention to this room, there will be consequences."

The guard pulled his hand from my mouth. I gulped in a huge breath of air, then sighed. "I know you're a good man," I said quietly, looking Kyle in the eye. "I know that you love Kelly more than life itself. And I know that she knows that."

Kyle nodded briefly. "Yes, I believe she does."

"But by letting this product go to market, you could be causing permanent damage to millions of young girls just like her!" I cried. "Maybe you're right. Maybe the toxin isn't really that dangerous. But what if it *is*? What if it causes paralysis or something worse to your consumers? Wouldn't you feel terrible?"

A shadow passed over Kyle's eyes, but he quickly recovered. "Nancy," he said, "this is a difficult world. Sometimes, in order to survive, we must take risks that make us uncomfortable." He swallowed. "I have identified what's most important to me, and that's my home life with Kelly, in our current lifestyle. I am willing to take risks to protect that lifestyle."

"But *you're* not taking the risk," I insisted, silently praying that I would get through to him. "You're forcing the risk onto millions of innocent consumers, all of them teenagers! Are you really willing to harm innocent strangers to keep—What? Your house, your fancy car?"

Kyle frowned, then cast his eyes downward. For a moment he seemed to be thinking over my question. I could feel my heart pounding in my chest as I awaited his answer. Was it possible? Could I change his mind? Was this our chance to stop Pretty Face from the inside?

But then, after a few seconds, Kyle's face seemed to close off. He raised his head, careful to avoid eye contact with me. "Please cover her mouth," he said simply to my guard. And just like that, a beefy hand was shoved over my lips and my glimmer of hope was extinguished.

"I am not a violent man," Kyle went on, raising his voice slightly. "I have never committed a crime before. I take no joy in others' pain."

I glanced at Anna. She swallowed hard. I don't think any of us liked where this speech was going.

"But you've left me no choice." Kyle regarded us all grimly. "After the pageant is over and our marketing campaign has been launched," he went on, "you will be escorted by my guards to a car. You will then be driven—"

Suddenly there was a commotion in the hallway. Giggling, and the patter of a gaggle of girls in high heels moving through the corridor to get backstage. There were murmurs and little comments—"Wow!" "My feet hurt." "Ugh, did you believe her answer?"—and then one voice rose above the others.

"Daddy?"

It was Kelly.

My heart sped up again. Kelly McMahon, one of the sweetest, most genuine people I'd ever met. Kelly McMahon, my New York roommate and pageant cheerleader. Kelly McMahon, Kyle's devoted daughter, who would surely be horrified to know what her father was doing in her name.

There was a light knock on the door. "Daddy? Did I just hear you in there?"

Kyle glanced at his guards, looking tense. "Take—"

But it was too late. Kelly pushed the door open and was confronted by a scene: the four of us, restrained and silenced by her father's personal security guards, and Kyle standing before us, in the middle of a speech.

Kelly's mouth dropped open. Her eyes widened

into saucers. "Daddy?" she asked again.

For a moment Kyle just stood there, stunned. All color drained from his face. I could tell he had never meant for Kelly to know what was going on with us, and he had no idea how to proceed. It took a few seconds for his color to return, but when it finally did, he turned to her with a saddened expression. "It's terrible, Kelly," he told her. "I know you trusted Nancy and her friends, but Nancy is reacting terribly to the investigation into the jewelry theft. She insists that she's meant to be Miss Pretty Face America, and is furious about ceding her place. . . . They're threatening to run out onstage to stop the pageant, causing a riot. . . . I had to subdue them. . . ."

Kelly looked utterly confused. I knew that she had found the jewelry in my luggage, and must have been struggling all day with the idea that I might be a thief. Still, we had spent enough time together for her to know her father's description of my behavior would be out of character, to say the least. She looked at me, pleadingly. Frustrated, I tried to convey my innocence with my eyes—*I would never do anything to deserve this treatment, Kelly*—but she turned back to her father, biting her lip.

"I'm shocked, Dad, but . . ."

I couldn't take it anymore. I bit down on my guard's hand with the force of a thousand pitbulls. I must have caught him off guard, because he squealed "Ow!" and pulled his hand away for just a second. It was enough for me to yell, "KELLY HE'S LYING! HE'S HOLDING US PRIS-ONER BECAUSE WE KNOW A SECRET ABOUT PER—"

The guard clamped his hand back over my mouth and pinched my arm, hard. "Behave!" he said gruffly.

Kelly started at me sadly, then shook her head, like she didn't know what to believe.

Kyle looked at Kelly, taking her hands and forc-ing her to face him. "She'll say anything, Kelly. We know she's a liar now. She already lied about being just another contestant, when, in fact, she was investigating us. You know me, Kelly. You know I'd be incapable of holding anyone—"

Kelly watched him, confused and sad. But as he went on pleading, she seemed to remember something. Before he could finish, she straight-ened up and asked pointedly, "What about Per-fect Face?"

Kyle seemed crushed, but he tried to keep his composure. "What about it?"

Kelly sighed. "If there's no secret . . . if Nancy

is lying . . . then why do you give me a different version of Perfect Face to use than the rest of the girls? Don't think I haven't noticed, Daddy. I'm not as naive as you think I am."

Kyle was silent. I could tell his mind was whirring, but he didn't know what to say. After a few seconds I could tell that it was too late, anyway. The hope on Kelly's face evaporated and was replaced by utter disappointment. In seconds, she went from being loving but concerned to the saddest I had ever seen her. She looked at her father with something resembling pity.

She took a deep breath, and before Kyle could respond she let out a bloodcurling scream. "HELP! POLICE! I NEED THE POLICE IN HERE! HELP ME!"

Chaos erupted. Kyle lunged to stop his daughter, but before he could do anything, uniformed officers came pouring in and broke up the scene. My mind was swimming as the police took in Kelly's version of the story and announced that we'd all have to be held for questioning to figure out exactly what had gone on in this room. Kyle looked utterly defeated, collapsing in a chair with his head in his hands. One of the policemen turned to me, frowning.

"Aren't you the pageant jewel thief?"

I sighed. "No," I said honestly. "I'm not."

Kelly edged closer. "I think Nancy may have been set up by my father, because of what she and her friends know," she said softly.

The cop looked skeptical. "You think your own father would set her up?"

Kelly nodded. "I do," she said sadly.

"And I can tell you that I haven't been at the hotel all day," I added. "You can check the security footage at the Pretty Face headquarters, and a taxi driver picked us up in Queens, and a coffee-shop owner . . . We were running around the city all day, trying to escape his goon." I gestured to Kyle.

"Well," said the cop slowly, turning from me to Kyle. "This has been a very interesting pageant so far."

"It's about to get more interesting," I promised, glancing at the TV screen, where Piper was belting out "Somewhere" from *West Side Story*. "I need to get to her sister in the audience," I said, pointing. "And I need to do it before I give my statement. I believe that she has evidence that could change the face of this whole case . . . and pageant."

11

AND THE WINNER IS . . .

"I believe that children are the future." Piper's voice boomed through the ballroom speakers as the security guard led Anna and I into the audience. Onstage, the girls had been whittled down to the top five semifinalists, and remarkably, Piper was one of them. She still wore her beautiful, sparkly violet evening gown from the River Heights pageant, and her makeup was perfect, making her dark eyes look huge and shiny.

"If we teach them well," Piper went on, "I believe they will lead the way. That is why I think we, as a country, need to focus on education. With a good education, every child can be shown the beauty he or she has inside."

The host, a game-show celebrity whose face appeared almost orange under the hot lights, smiled a crinkly smile. "Thank you, Miss River Heights. Is my card correct here? Were you, in fact, the runner-up in your regional pageant?"

For just a second a murderous expression passed across Piper's face, but she recovered quickly. "That's correct," she said. "The winner of the title, Nancy Drew, turned out to be a liar and a thief. I guess it just goes to show, you can't judge a book by its cover." She smiled a million-kilowatt smile.

The host smiled too. "Well, River Heights is certainly fortunate to have such a lovely and talented runner-up. Miss River Heights, why don't you take your place among the five semifinalists."

Piper nodded and gracefully walked back to the platform where the other contestants were waiting.

Meanwhile the guard had led us to an intersection of aisles, and frowned, searching through the dark audience. "This way," he said, pointing, and we followed.

"Ladies and gentlemen," intoned the host, "it is now time to say good-bye to more lovely contestants. I hold in my hands the list of three finalists, one of whom will be this year's Miss Pretty Face!" He paused, and the audience erupted in applause. "The finalists are . . . Miss San Jose!" More applause; screaming from Miss San Jose. "Miss Tampa!" More applause; even more screaming. "And Miss River Heights!"

"Oh my god!" a voice cried from only feet away. I turned toward the source of the sound, and there she was: Robin Depken, our only hope of showing evidence of Pretty Face's wrongdoing. She was dressed in a prim, gray pantsuit, with her pale hair gathered in a bun, clapping like crazy and totally engrossed with her sister's stroll to center stage.

"Robin," Anna hissed as we paused at her aisle.

Robin glanced at us, then away, then did a double take. *"Anna?"* Then she spotted me behind her friend. "Nancy Drew? I thought you were . . ."

"Miss," the guard broke in insistently. "We need you to come speak with us at the rear of the auditorium. It will only take a minute."

Robin frowned. "But my sister is one of the three finalists! If she wins, I want to be here."

The guard sighed.

"Robin," Anna whispered, "trust me, this is very important."

Robin frowned, looking skeptical. But after a

few seconds, she awkwardly looked around her and got to her feet. "All right," she whispered, sliding by the other audience members in her aisle. "But just for a minute!"

We walked to the back of the ballroom, out of earshot of the audience members. When we all turned to face one another, everyone wore a different expression: the guard, skepticism; Robin, confusion; Anna, determination; and me, hope.

"Robin," Anna began, "I'm going to cut to the chase. Did you set me up?"

Robin looked stunned. *"What?"* she asked. "I don't know what you're talking about. If anything, I thought *you* set *me* up."

"What?" I asked, totally lost.

"Wait a minute, wait a minute, wait a minute," Anna insisted, gesturing for us to all calm down. "Robin, I gave you a flash drive full of evidence against Pretty Face cosmetics. Less than an hour later, I was grabbed off the street, taken to Pretty Face headquarters, drugged, and held prisoner for two days." She paused. "It was only when Nancy came looking for me, and after they moved us to an offsite research facility, that we were able to escape."

Robin looked totally surprised. "Wow," she whispered.

Anna continued, "We've spent the whole day trying to keep one step ahead of Pretty Face and their goons," she said. "Now we're safe, but we need your help. Do you have the flash drive I gave you, Robin? If so, we need it right now."

Robin swallowed. "Wow," she repeated softly. "Wow. No, I—When I met with you, Anna, you told me you were going right to the press," she said. "And of course I supported you. Pretty Face cosmetics ruined my life. They took away my position as runner-up last year, they took my scholarship money—everything."

She paused. "I've been working three jobs, trying to pay for school. So when you said you were going to take them down, Anna, I was all for it."

Robin sighed. "But then you disappeared, and I never saw anything in the press. Maybe it was naive of me, but I blamed *you*, Anna, for your own disappearance. I thought maybe your meeting with me had been recorded or videotaped, that you were trying to capture me plotting against Pretty Face in the hopes of pushing Piper out of the competition!"

Anna scoffed.

"It's not so crazy, Anna," Robin insisted. "Think about it. Pretty Face tricked me in some pretty underhanded ways. And you worked for

Pretty Face. I thought they were trying to knock the Depkens out of competition, once and for all."

Anna shook her head. "I would never, Robin—never—plot with Pretty Face against you. You're my friend. I trusted you."

Robin sighed and looked down at her feet. "I'm sorry I didn't go look for you."

I broke in. "Look, it's all right. You're just friends who misunderstood each other. Please, all that matters now is that you still have that flash drive."

Robin bit her lip. "Oh Anna."

Anna looked alarmed. "What is it?" she demanded.

Robin looked from me to Anna, tears glistening in her dark eyes. "It's gone," she whispered. "It was stolen from Piper's and my hotel room. I thought it was Piper's Pretty Face chaperones. They must have seen it and figured out what it was."

Onstage, Piper was beaming into the microphone. "If I win Miss Pretty Face," she was saying, "I promise to represent my generation with pride! Beauty, freshness, and integrity—that's what young people today are all about!"

"Robin," I said abruptly, "Did anyone else

know about your meeting with Anna?"

Robin shrugged. "Not really," she replied. "I left a note for Piper that morning, just to let her know I'd gone to a nearby diner for breakfast. I didn't say I was meeting anyone."

All the contestants had retreated to their little platform at the front of the stage and were holding hands and wiggling with anticipation. The host was halfway through his speech about this being it, and what the Miss Pretty Face crown entailed, and how this girl's life would change, etc., etc.

"The second runner-up is . . . ," he concluded. "Miss Tampa!"

Cheers and squeals. Piper and Miss San Jose hugged each other, but their eyes never left the host. Piper's smile took up half her face, but her eyes were cold. Impatiently waiting.

And then it came to me.

"And the first runner-up is . . . ," the host continued, "Miss San Jose! That means our new Miss Pretty Face America is—"

Before anyone could stop me, I began charging down the center aisle, running too fast and with too much power for anyone to dissuade me from my ultimate goal. I heard Anna cry "Nancy?!" behind me, and the guard's heavy footsteps following me, but I kept charging forward. Shoving past the security guard, who tried to grab me and missed, I ran up the steps to the stage, charged to the center platform where the stunned host stood speechless, and grabbed the mic.

"WAIT!" I cried, facing a sea of confused, angry-looking faces. "Stop the show! This pageant is a scam!!"

PERFECT CONCLUSION

"Okay," the sandy-haired policeman, who I now knew was named Officer Kilkelly, said patiently. "Now that the chaos has ended, and we're all settled here backstage with some time to think . . . Nancy, tell us again what you think happened."

I took a deep breath, looking around at the assembled faces; some hostile, some encouraging, like Bess, George, and Anna, who circled me. "Robin," I began, turning to Anna's ally who sat across from me, "I believe you when you say you only meant to help Anna and didn't set her up. I believe that your sister, Piper, saw your note about eating breakfast at the diner and went to meet you." I paused. Piper, who was sitting next to her sister with some serious attitude showing on her face, scoffed. She'd been *beyond* furious to have her moment of victory interrupted by me and made into a public scandal.

"Okay, Nancy," she said, rolling her eyes. "Last I checked, it was no crime to have *breakfast* with my *sister.*"

"I'm not finished," I replied coolly, turning to Officer Kilkelly. "Piper never met up with her sister. Because once she got to the diner, she saw that her sister was actually having breakfast with Anna Chavez. A few minutes of eavesdropping was enough to convince her she had enough juicy information to succeed where her sister had failed: She could use the information about the frog toxin to blackmail Pretty Face into giving her the crown!"

Piper looked stunned, but I was pretty sure she was stunned to be *caught*, and not by my accusations. "That's . . . that's . . . Are you saying I'm not a strong enough contestant to win on my own?"

I looked at her. "I'm saying you've been obsessed with winning this pageant ever since you became a serious contender in River Heights, and Piper, I think you're just ruthless enough to resort to blackmail." I paused. "Besides, it explains what happened to the flash drive." I turned back to Officer Kilkelly. "When Robin met with Anna, Anna gave her a flash drive filled with incriminating evidence against Pretty Face. Robin took it back to her room, where Piper swiped it and set up a meeting with Kyle McMahon. I'm betting that she made some sort of deal with him. She would give him the flash drive as soon as she was wearing the Miss Pretty Face America crown."

Piper swallowed. "That's ridiculous! I just wanted to compete fair and square to represent my generation!"

Officer Kilkelly looked skeptical. "Okay, there's one important piece of information missing from your explanation," he said. "What's on the flash drive?"

I looked to Anna.

"Well," she said slowly, "Officer Kilkelly, I've been working for Pretty Face for a few years. I've watched them develop the new product they introduced at the pageant—Perfect Face, a new moisturizer and revitalizer."

Officer Kilkelly nodded. "I'm sure my daughter will be asking for it tomorrow," he said warily.

"What makes Perfect Face special . . . ," Anna continued, glancing at Kyle, who watched her with steely eyes from the seat next to Officer

Kilkelly, "is one ingredient. It's a toxin extracted from the *unibro* frog, native to Venezuela."

Officer Kilkelly wrinkled his nose. "Okay, that's a little gross but not illegal."

"Let me explain," Anna said, sitting up in her chair. "The toxin isn't Botox, but it has similar, less extreme effects. With repeated use, it firms the skin and gives a healthy glow. The problem is, in Venezuela, the indigenous people avoid using the toxin on their face, because they believe over time it can lead to paralysis and even death."

Officer Kilkelly looked skeptical. "Pretty Face is a well-respected company," he said. "I'm sure they safety tested—"

Anna shook her head. "That's where you're wrong. Over and over I tried to make the corporation aware of the risks, to convince them to fund a long-term study. But over and over they refused. Other companies had learned about this toxin, and Pretty Face wanted to rush it to market before the competition came out."

Officer Kilkelly turned to Kyle, frowning. "Is that true?"

Kyle shook his head, staring into his lap. "It's perfectly safe," he replied. "Perfect Face is perfectly safe. We didn't take any unnecessary risks. These ladies have no proof."

"Not now," I agreed, "but I think we can find proof pretty easily." I glanced at Piper, who scowled.

Officer Kilkelly turned to me. "And where do you think we can find this proof?"

I smiled. "I'd suggest starting with Piper's dressing station. If she agreed to hand over the flash drive after winning, that means the flash drive must be somewhere in this hotel."

Seconds later we were all crowded around Piper's dressing station. The other pageant contestants had been corralled into a large sitting area backstage, and they watched us curiously as we all trooped from the small sitting room to the area where the girls had gotten dressed. Piper's station—what had actually been *my* station during rehearsals, before I went to find Anna and got involved in one of the scariest adventures of my life—was covered with cosmetics, a good luck teddy bear, and a photo of Piper and a handsome boy her age. It was just like every other dressing station in the hotel, but I believed important evidence was hidden within.

Officer Kilkelly and his two colleagues worked quickly. They pulled open the drawers and dumped the contents onto the floor, picking through them with their hands. One drawer, two drawers, nothing. But then the third drawer was emptied, and one of the officers stopped in his search. "What's this?" he asked, holding up a plain cardboard box.

Piper scowled. She seemed unusually on edge. "It's just *lotion*," she scoffed, shrugging and rolling her eyes. "Jeez."

The officer opened the box and took out a small, plain bottle of white lotion. Taped to the front was a handwritten label: "Perfect Face."

It was the same version Kyle had given Kelly.

"Boss," said one of the other officers, picking up a tiny object. "Look at this."

It was tiny—too tiny, you'd think, to hold such important information. I made a mental note to ask George later just how these tiny flash drives worked. Made of translucent orange plastic, just big enough for a USB connection, the flash drive was attached to a cord you could wear around your neck. It had been buried at the bottom of the drawer, under a mountain of cosmetics.

"Well, well, well," Officer Kilkelly said, taking the flash drive and glancing sideways at Piper, who was looking away with wet eyes. "I think we'd better head over to the hotel business center and check this out."

A few minutes later, we were all crowded around a desktop computer in the hotel's small business center. One of Officer Kilkelly's colleagues, Officer Pirelli, plugged the flash drive into the USB port.

Within seconds, folders of data popped up on the screen. Officer Pirelli clicked on one labeled EMAILS NOVEMBER–DECEMBER.

Kyle—

I don't think you understand the importance of what I'm suggesting. If the indigenous people are right and the toxin can cause paralysis over time, then we are potentially freezing the faces of countless customers! You can see from the article I sent that I'm not the only one with these concerns. Please tell me we will fund a long-term study. It's the responsible thing to do.

Best,
Anna

Anna,

This is none of your concern. I've heard your evidence, now drop it. We certainly are not going to derail a multimillion dollar product launch because a few poor folks in Venezuela got sick. Who knows what caused their paralysis? Who knows what they eat? If you value your job, don't bring this matter to me again. We have made our decision.

—Kyle

Kyle,
Please, please reconsider. Reread the article I sent you. I know you are a moral person.
Anna

Anna,
Drop it, now. The next contact you receive from me on this matter will be your walking papers.
Kyle

"Wow," Officer Pirelli muttered, looking from the computer screen to Kyle. "I'd say that's pretty clear evidence that you knew of the dangers. Kyle McMahon, you're under arrest. We'd better take you and Piper down to the station and look into the matter further. You have the right to remain silent . . ."

As Officer Pirelli read Kyle his Miranda rights, which I was all too familiar with, Officer Kilkelly and the third officer, Officer Kouletsis, handcuffed Kyle and Piper. Robin started crying, sobbing, "Why, Piper? I knew I should have never let you enter the pageant. . . ."

Anna shot a victorious glance at me, and Bess hugged me. "Great work, Nance," she said with a big smile. "I know of at least *one* pretty face you saved from being frozen in place!"

George was smiling too. "Not bad at all," she agreed. "It's just too bad this took so long, and you had to miss the pageant."

I scowled at her. As Piper and Kyle were led out of the room in handcuffs, Officer Kikelly turned to me. "How did you put all this together?" he asked. "You were a contestant. But it seems like you'd be a better candidate for Miss Amateur Detective."

"That's me," I agreed with a sigh. "Unfortunately I think that's the only pageant title I have a real shot at."

"Well, I knew New York would be exciting," Bess said, stretching out on Kelly's double bed in our hotel room. "I just didn't know *how* exciting."

"Yeah, Nance," George agreed, slipping the metal cover back over her room-service plate. We'd ordered in burgers for dinner, having seen enough of New York City for one day. "You're quite the little tour guide. Better than those double-decker bus tours, I'm sure."

"Ohhhh," Bess moaned with a little pout. "I wanted to take one of those."

"Next time," I said. "By noon tomorrow, we'll be back in River Heights."

"And not a moment too soon," George added. "No offense to the Big Apple."

Bess sighed. "No, I agree." She frowned. "I never thought I'd want to quit thrilling New York City for quiet little River Heights, but I think I've had enough excitement for . . . well, for at least this week."

"Agreed," I said.

"Agreed," echoed George. "Maybe someday we'll come back for a vacation. But right now, I think I just want to sleep and watch bad reality television for a week."

"Wow," Bess murmured. "You know it's serious when George wants to watch reality TV."

"Oh my gosh," George murmured. "A full day, a bag of Doritos and a reality TV marathon? That's where I am right now. That's what you've turned me into, Nancy."

I grabbed a pillow from the edge of the bed we were lounging on and tossed it at her. "Don't blame me. Blame Pretty Face cosmetics."

"Guys," I said, sitting up on the bed as a thought occurred to me, "in case I didn't say it at the time, thank you, *thank you* for coming after me this morning. If you guys hadn't cracked the Hyungkoo43 code, I'd still be moldering away in a basement in Queens."

Bess and George looked at me sympathetically. "Don't mention it," said George.

"Yeah, thank you for saving our lives by setting the hotel room on fire," Bess added, then shook her head. "Gosh, that sounds weird."

"We don't know what Adam Bedrossian would have done to us," George murmured.

I shuddered. "I don't want to think about it." When we'd all gone down to the police station for further questioning, we'd learned that Adam Bedrossian had been arrested at our hotel for arson and illegal possession of a firearm. So we had outsmarted him, in a way, even before we proved to the NYPD that Pretty Face was guilty of some serious crimes. That felt pretty good.

We were quiet for a few seconds, then a few minutes. It felt so good to lie down and feel safe. So good . . .

"I'm falling asleep," Bess said after a couple of minutes. "Guys, I think it's time we break up the party. We should go to bed anyway. We're going to have to get up bright and early to make our flight home."

"Good idea," George agreed, and slowly, clearly not enjoying it, they pulled themselves off Kelly's bed and got to their feet. Reluctantly I followed suit.

"Any word from Kelly?" George asked as I walked them to the door.

I shook my head sadly. "Last I heard she was still at the police station," I replied. "Her boyfriend had come to support her, though. She was pretty shaken up."

Bess nodded. "It must be terrible to learn that the person you trust most in the world is capable of something like this," she said.

I nodded. "Definitely. But Kelly's strong. I hope she'll be okay."

We said our good nights, and in the quiet room, I changed into my pjs and slipped into bed. Leaving the front light on for Kelly, I closed my eyes and thought of home, Dad, Hannah, and Ned. Hannah's homemade cookies. My own bed . . .

"Nancy?"

The next thing I knew, I woke up and spotted Kelly putting her purse down on the bedside table. "I'm sorry. I tried to be quiet so I wouldn't wake you."

"No, no," I insisted, blinking and sitting up in bed. "No, I wanted to be woken. What time is it?"

Kelly sighed. "It's late. A little past one." She paused, looking down at her hands. "Andrew took me out for a late dinner at a diner. I think I needed some time to wind down."

I bit my lip. Even though I knew it wasn't my fault Kyle had turned to the dark side, I still felt guilty for being the one who busted him. "Kelly, I'm so sorry."

"Don't be." Kelly shook her head. "My father made his own decisions. He decided he was okay with hurting people for his own gain. I don't understand it, but I don't blame you, Nancy. You were only doing what was right."

"Either way," I said, "I'm so sorry for what you're going through."

Kelly smiled a tiny smile. "Thanks," she replied. "It's hard, Nancy, but I'll be okay. I called my aunt who lives here in New York, and she's just as surprised and shaken up by this as I am. I think I may stay here for a while with her."

I nodded. "It's good to have someone to lean on."

"Right." Kelly smiled again. "And maybe this will give me the kick in the butt I need to go back to school. Andrew is at NYU, and I might apply to join him next semester." She paused. "Up till now, my life has been so tied up with Dad's. I lived at home, because I wanted to keep him company. I joined the pageant, because he thought it would be good for me." She sighed. "Maybe it's time I got my own life and started making *me* happy."

I smiled. "That sounds like a great idea, Kelly. You told me a while back you were interested in being a doctor. I think you'd be a great one."

Kelly nodded. "Thanks, Nance. Anything's possible. I've only ruled out one thing."

"What's that?" I asked.

Kelly laughed. "I'm definitely done with pageants for good."

"Is this the sort of romantic dinner you had in mind?"

I couldn't help but smile as my boyfriend, Ned, took my hand and whispered to me as we moved into his dining room for dinner. We'd been apart for a week, since I'd been on a super complicated case that brought me to New York, and had planned to make tonight our official "catch-up date" at our favorite Italian restaurant. But this afternoon Ned had called with a change in plans. There'd been a mix-up with faculty housing at the university, so he volunteered to host a visiting professor from Iran and his family at the Nickerson home. Ned and his parents wanted to have a small dinner to welcome them, and tonight was the only night that worked for everyone.

I leaned in close to him. "Romance, shromance. A piece of your mother's apple pie will make up for anything we missed."

Ned chuckled and squeezed my hand. "Maybe so. But we'll have to plan a makeup date."

"Agreed." I squeezed back and smiled.

The truth was, it still felt nice to be back in River Heights and doing all the normal things I like to do that don't involve cab chases or setting things on fire. My most recent case had turned into something bigger and crazier than I ever could have anticipated, and I was enjoying being "Normal Nancy" again, instead of "Action Hero Nancy." Being back in

Ned's house felt wonderful. And the Nickersons' new houseguests—Professor Mirza Al-Fulani; his daughter, Arij, who was twelve; and his son, Ibrahim, who was sixteen—just couldn't be nicer.

"So Nancy," Ibrahim began with a smile as we sat down at the dining room table, "have your travels for investigations ever taken you out of the country? Have you been to the Middle East at all?"

I smiled. The Al-Fulanis were from Iran, and I was enjoying Ibrahim's upbeat attempts to understand American culture. "I'm afraid not, Ibrahim. I don't get the chance to travel all that much, even within the U.S. But I would love to visit the Middle East someday. There's so much history there."

Professor Al-Fulani smiled at me. "This is true, Nancy. It is still sometimes strange for my children and me to wrap our heads around American history, because your country is so new. So much has changed in only two hundred years, whereas in our part of the world, there are thousands of years of history."

Ibrahim piped up excitedly. "Will we study American history at the high school, Nancy?"

I nodded. "Actually, you will, Ibrahim. It's a required class for juniors."

"Excellent." Ibrahim dug into his salad with a grin, glancing at his sister. "I want to learn as much as I can about this country while we are here. I am so eager to meet my classmates."

Arij smiled and nodded, glancing at Ned and I. "Maybe you could look at the outfit I plan to wear tomorrow, Nancy," she said shyly. "I want to fit in well, and make friends quickly."

I laughed. "I don't know if I'm the best person to give fashion advice, but I'd be happy to offer my opinion."

Ned squeezed my arm. "Don't sell yourself short, Nance," he cautioned. "After all, you are the reigning Miss Pretty Face River Heights!"

I rolled my eyes at him. While that was true, I wasn't exactly aching to talk about my short and ill-fated career as a pageant queen, which had been part of the case I'd been investigating in New York. Still, he was smiling. I knew he found my totally out-of-character pageant win amusing.

"Nancy," Ibrahim said again, "I am curious about how you solve cases. Ned told us a little about your unusual hobby earlier, and I must ask: Do you wear disguises? Do you ever have to lie to people to get the information you need?"

I squirmed in my seat. Ibrahim's face was warm and open, and I knew his questions were coming from an honest curiosity. Still, I liked to keep my trade secrets, and didn't exactly want to confess to bending the truth in the service of, well, the truth, in front of Ned's father and a bunch of people I'd just met.

"Let's just say I do what the case requires," I replied, reaching out for the bread basket. "Every case is different. More bread, anybody?"

Mrs. Nickerson chuckled.

"Ibrahim and Arij," Ned cut in smoothly, "have you ever been to an American high school before, or will tomorrow be your first time?"

"Oh no," Ibrahim replied, shaking his head. "We have attended school in America before. My father travels often for work, you know, and we have traveled with him for months at a time."

Professor Al-Fulani nodded. "My children lived with me while I taught at a university in Wisconsin, and also briefly in Florida. Unfortunately, both placements were only for a few months, so they weren't able to settle in as they would have liked."

Arij nodded, pushing her salad around on her plate. "Sometimes it's hard to make friends," she admitted, a note of sadness creeping into her voice. "People hear my accent or they see my headscarf and they think— they think I am something that I am not."

Silence bloomed around the table. I nodded sympathetically, imagining how difficult it must be for Arij and Ibrahim to fit in.

"I don't think that will be the case here, Arij," Ned said in a warm voice. "At least, I hope not. We're a university town, and used to diversity."

Mr. Nickerson cleared his throat. "You have any trouble, Arij or Ibrahim, and you let me know," he agreed. "Ned and I will do everything we can to make your stay here as pleasant as possible."

Arij smiled. She looked a little relieved. "I can't wait to meet everyone," she said quietly.

"Ibrahim and Arij seem very nice," I said to Ned a couple of hours later, as we stood on his porch to say our good-nights. "I think they'll enjoy living here, don't you? I think they'll have a good experience at the high school."

Ned nodded. "I hope so. They're definitely a couple of great kids—so friendly and curious. I think as long as their classmates give them a chance, they'll have plenty of friends."

I nodded. The night was growing darker, and crickets chirped in the distance. I took a deep breath. River Heights, I thought happily. Home.

"So . . . ," Ned began, reaching out to squeeze my hand.

"So," I agreed, looking up at him with a smile. "Dinner? Later this week? Just the two of us?"

Ned grinned and nodded. "I'll call you," he agreed, leaning over to give me a peck on the cheek. "I'm so glad you're back, safe and sound."

"Me too," I said honestly, squeezing his hand again.

"Thank your mom for dinner. It was delicious."

Stepping down to the driveway, I pulled out the keys to my hybrid car and felt a wave of exhaustion wash over me. I imagined my nice warm bed at home, beckoning me. Without a case or anything urgent on the agenda, I could sleep in a bit tomorrow too. I sighed, driving carefully through the streets that led me home. What a relief to be home among the people I loved, and with a little downtime.

At home, I parked the car in our driveway and yawned as I walked around to the back door. I felt like I had tunnel vision—all I could see was the route to my bedroom, where I'd soon be off to dreamland. Which is why I didn't notice that the kitchen light was on. And three people were sitting at the kitchen table, watching me curiously.

"Nancy?"

A familiar voice pulled me out of my tunnel vision, and I turned to find an unusual sight: my friend Bess; her little sister, Maggie; and our housekeeper and unofficial member of the family, Hannah; were munching on oatmeal raisin cookies.

"Bess?" I asked, walking in. What on earth?

Bess stood, placing her hand on Maggie's shoulder. "We were waiting for you to come home," she said. "Hope you're not too tired, Nance. Because I think we've got a case for you."

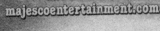